Mario 2

Coming of Age

Works by George Hatcher
One Wilshire

Fiction by George Hatcher

Ambulance Chaser Series
Mario 1: Woman in Jeopardy
Mario 2: Coming of Age
Mario 3: Risky Business
Mario 4: Ambulance Chaser (2017)
Mario 5: Jack the Banker (2017)
Mario 6: Flyboy (2017)
*Upcoming Titles may change

Independent Titles
Arabe (2017)
Pretty Face (2017)

CasaHatcherPress Pasadena

To Molly.
My partner.
My friend.
My wife of 50 years, with all
the love my soul can generate.

To Jody, my legal assistant in my other job. When we think we're ready for press, Jody comes in like a stalking cat and catches a whole mess of mistakes.

To Allie, my collaborator and chief editor, without whom I would be lost for sure.

Mario is a work of fiction. It is purely a product of long, boring plane flights leading to flights of fantasy, the wild goose chasing of a caffeine-fueled imagination, and a dull foundation of years of experience doing a job that is not terribly unlike Mario's. If this seems to resemble someone you know or think you know, then I have done my job.

Prologue
1972

His name was Mario Luna. Some people called him an ambulance chaser, though he'd never chased an ambulance in his life. He was not a lawyer, but without all the lawyers he knew who relied on him, he'd have no job. His name was on doors inside law firms, but mostly he worked out of his car. His weapon was a quick tongue, a cool head, miles of street cunning, and a well-earned degree from the school of hard knocks. He almost always scored his man, but he didn't work alone. He had a vast network composed of street people, white collar workers, everyday folks who called him when they sniffed something he'd be interested in. He was generous with these chatty friends, whether they were ambulance drivers or hot nurses who met him in motels to exchange saliva and secrets. There were a million folks who came across accident victims and their families. They left him messages on his answering machine. Some called his beeper and didn't leave a word. Just the call, and he'd recognize the number, and cruise the emergency room, or funeral home, or body shop where they worked.

It was not as easy as it sounded, though there were more than a couple of his friends who were very good and practically had his clients signed before he was even in the picture. If his relationship with his "scouts" was good, his relationship with clients was better. What made the difference was how much he cared. There was the challenge of business, and his drive to win, but what it really came down to was people. He was all about the people. And the angles, too, of course. He was good at that. He'd been working angles for a long time, his whole life, in fact.

Chapter 1
(1959)

Liquid red sprayed, splayed, played, shimmered and sashayed. Strings of color dribbled down, dragged by their own weight, in reluctant obedience to gravity. Targeted up close, the spray made a tiny, heavy circle, but widened into a finer glaze with every inch that he stepped back. Interesting. Mario relaxed his finger, flexed, and held it down again. A fresh stream overlay the first, merged, dripped. It wasn't graffiti. It was a symphony in red.

"Looks like blood," Pélon said, watching a drip coagulate. "My turn." Pélon snatched the can and shook it, judging its weight. Mario did not protest, though he had nothing to show for the whole spray can adventure but a red-painted finger. It had been fun, sure. Now the evidence needed to be removed from his skin before school, or he'd never hear the end of it. Besides, Pélon had earned the can. He'd stolen it fair and square from Pélon's mother's latest squeeze, a down-and-out house painter who had not let Pélon's tender age immunize him from giving him the gift of two black eyes. They weren't black yet, but they would be within twenty-four hours. Pélon had not paid cash for the stolen paint, but in currency of his own blood.

The huge wooden crate the boys had found weeks ago and dragged here had once housed a sofa now residing in one of the surrounding shops. After they hammered the pried-off planks back together and made rope hinges for a door, they rolled the crate over so now the door was an awning propped open with the end of a discarded broom handle. Inside were assorted treasures, including a broken shelf, a candle, an old bag of popcorn, and homework that Pélon had forgotten to bring with him to school. The floor was covered entirely by mismatched sofa cushions and pillows that were the aftermath of Pélon's last eviction, plus abandoned stuff from the family that used to live in 13b who had quit paying rent and slipped away quietly in the night.

This was their first clubhouse, but they hadn't let Carson in on it yet.

Mario admired the shiny red adorning the otherwise dull brick, not wanting to be late for school, not really wanting to go, either, and not wanting to bring up the topic.

"What time was it when you left the house?"

Pélon shrugged. "I didn't look at the clock."

"Yeah," Mario laughed. "Your Pop nearly nabbed you."

"He's not my Pop!" Pélon yelled, dropped the can, and launched himself at Mario.

"Okay, okay!" Well aware of the revolving partners behind those particular closed doors, Mario had spoken without thinking, never a wise approach to Pélon who was apt to go gonzo at the slightest provocation. "Pop" had been meant as sarcasm, since the boyfriends usually told Pélon to call them Pop, or Dad, but for such a tough kid, he was remarkably thin-skinned.

"Okay" was clearly inadequate for an apology, and without delay, Pélon started pummeling. Mario curled up and covered his head, ready for the long haul because Pélon was a teaspoon of a boy with a cup full of rage, but before he found his rhythm, Pélon's weight was lifted from his body.

The shopkeeper set Pélon aside and loomed close. Mario had frequently seen the little Oriental shopkeeper people-watching in the doorway of his shop on Brooklyn, but never before inches from his face. Pélon, however, was not deterred. He'd already been tossed down one set of stairs that morning, and the little stranger hadn't even drawn blood. He grabbed the can, and rolled to his feet.

Mario had a close-up view as the shopkeeper saw the paint on his formerly spotless wall. He recognized the look of dismay as it crossed the hundred creases in the old man's face, and felt a wash of guilt, though he never understood why adults cared about walls anyway. Pélon raised the hand with the can.

"No!" Mario said, though it wasn't as if Pélon were the type who listened. By the time the words were out of his mouth, it was too late, anyway. Pélon had already blasted the shopkeeper in the face with red.

"Vamos!"

Pélon tore out of the alley, Mario hot on his heels. Behind them, the little Oriental jabbered furiously in Chinese, Japanese, or Korean, but they didn't stop running. The second flight of the day, and it wasn't even eight yet.

How the morning had begun:

Mario, who was never good at waiting, had gone to Pélon's side of the building. They usually walked to school together on the days that Pélon actually went to school. He knew before he turned the corner this would not be one of those waiting days, because he could already hear the screaming. On screaming days, Pélon was highly motivated to make a quick getaway. Pélon's mother and her latest boyfriend aimed their voices like shotguns, fired them off like soldiers in a war zone, and woe be to anyone who got in the way. The neighborhood responded accordingly.

Pélon must have been watching at the window for Mario's arrival, because Mario had barely caught sight of the rusted space where the building's numbers used to be when the battered door to the apartment burst open. Pélon dashed out like the devil was after him and tore past Mario. Before he took off for points unknown, without breaking stride, he made a dive for a sad bush in what passed for the front yard and grabbed what looked like a can of hair spray hidden underneath.

Then he was gone.

The slamming door interrupted a screaming match inside the house, and the altercation moved outdoors. A man stepped out. The one Mario had called "Pop" was a burly fellow, his face half-covered in shaving cream. Shirtless, hairy, heavily tattooed. Mario had never seen him up close, but this "pop" had only been around a week or two. He had the stocky build, smashed face, and snarl of an angry bulldog, which Mario was able to observe close up because the stranger did not stop till he reached the sidewalk. He was followed closely by Pélon's mom, a frail birdlike creature with a voice like a foghorn, and more mascara than brains, as Mario's aunt used to say.

"Good morning, Mario."

Pélon's mom acknowledged him, then turned her attention to coaxing the man inside. She called him Martin. Stubbornly, Martin looked both ways down the street as if the running boy would magically and stupidly reappear. He allowed himself to be led inside, swearing all the way, his paint-stained hand and arm draped over the little woman's shoulder like an old sweater knit of leftover yarn. Technically Mario was alone on the street, but he pretended not to see the faces and ears pressed to every window. It was not unusual for the chaos at Pélon's house to provide entertainment for the entire thin-walled neighborhood.

Knowing the scene would get back to his aunt, he shouted, "I'm going straight to school!" Then he headed off in search of Pélon. Even after the graffiti episode, he'd have made it to the class on time—if he hadn't stopped in the bathroom to try to scrub the paint off his finger.

Mario was ten, and for as long as he could recall, had lived in a two bedroom apartment on Chicago Street in East Los Angeles. He lived with his Aunt Carmen who really was his aunt. He knew that his mother's name was Elena, and that Elena was Auntie's sister, and that Elena was in heaven. She had died when he was born, because she was too beautiful for this earth, and God wanted her in heaven. Auntie was always wagging her finger in his face, saying she had secrets he didn't want to know, and if he didn't straighten up and fly right, she'd tell him. She was very worried about the devil in Mario, and so they went to church. A lot.

He vaguely recalled an Uncle Moonie who could reach up and touch the ceiling without standing on his toes. He was loud and laughed, and even made Aunt Carmen laugh, but that was from a dim time before they had moved to Chicago street. Now Uncle Moonie only showed up in nightmares.

Mario asked his aunt why the other kids said he was a bastard. Not that they were trying to be mean, but it was a neighborhood fact, and he'd seen for himself, when aunties had babies they raised, they had no daddy, and neither did Mario. One time she got drunk, she told him his middle name was Sanchez, and that it was a secret between God and Carmen, because if he was a bastard, it was because his father was a bastard, not because he was really a bastard. Mario told her that confused him, so she promised him on her Bible that he wasn't a bastard. His mother and his father had really been married. He knew that was the truth, because she'd never lie on the Bible. He wouldn't have minded being Aunt Carmen's bastard since he didn't really know the legendary beautiful Elena, but he sure knew Aunt Carmen. Everyone came to Aunt Carmen for advice, but Mario didn't ask her nosy questions after that, not sure if she was crazy or if she was right that the stuff she wanted to keep secret really was stuff he was better off not knowing.

He knew his mother had been beautiful. His aunt put a picture of her on top of his dresser so he would never forget her. His aunt told him how his mother had died when he was born, and was very vague about his father. Apart from the secrets in his aunt's stories about stuff he couldn't recall, she was very open with him. They lived okay, just like everybody in the apartments where they lived. Like everybody, when the budget was right, she got new furniture for their small apartment. She even ordered a television set, which only a few of his friends had at home. It was black and white. His aunt did all this working for $1.10 per hour at a sewing factory, and sometimes midwifing babies, especially for poor neighbors soon-to-become aunties. (She used to be a nurse, and had the papers to prove it.) He loved that furniture store downtown where his auntie had an account, mainly because they let them have what they bought on credit. It was called Dearden's and they even stocked the new color televisions. He had watched one while Auntie was shopping, and tried to talk her into buying it, but Auntie said it cost too much.

His aunt could not explain how the picture in the box could come from a roof antenna and a wire. He didn't even want to think about how a color picture would come down the same way. He had more questions than Carter had liver pills, and hated so much not to understand.

Auntie was still at work when the Dearden's guy rang the bell to deliver the television. At that very moment, Mario had been in his closet with a blanket over his head and a flashlight in his hand, about to look at the secret magazines Big Juan loaned him. Big Juan had only given him fifteen minutes and was coming back to get them before his father got home. The bell sent him into a panic, but he shoved them under his bed and opened the door to a round guy with a rolling laugh and a huge belly that strained his buttons. Mario recognized the Dearden's label on his shirt and let him in. Big Juan came in right after and asked where his workbook was from Algebra class. Mario knew he meant the magazines.

"They're on my bed," Mario said, pointing. He didn't leave the front room, where the Dearden's guy was. His aunt had told him to "keep an eye on things." The magazines were under his bed, but that would have sounded weird. Why would he put Juan's Algebra workbook under his bed?

"That big kid is in your class? You take algebra?" the Dearden's guy asked.

He wasn't really in Mario's class. He was a much older boy from around the neighborhood. Mario didn't even know if he was still in school. He didn't want to lie, so he whispered very quietly, "He's not very smart," which was the truth.

Juan left with the magazines after taking about ten minutes to find them.

The two Dearden's guys went down to their truck and came back up, both complaining about the steps. There weren't many stairs on the first floor, but Mario knew from experience that when you weren't paying attention, the two little ones between the walk and the corridor were apt to trip you up. Mario had shut the door, but let them back in, watching as they carried the TV between them, and dropped it loudly on the floor.

"I'm tired of being the one to do the antenna. You should do it some-time."

"I make too big a hole when I fall off the roof," the fat guy chuckled.

"It's hot as the devil's pitchfork," the grouchy one complained and went outside into the heat, not laughing. They could hear him thumping the ladder and bumping about all the way to the roof.

"He sure is grouchy," Mario said. "How come?"

"Because I'm too fat to get on the ladder, and he has to do it," the big guy said. "But his job is to go up there and make the antenna stick to the roof. He doesn't know how to do anything else, and he's too dumb to learn."

"Why?"

"Because he quit school too soon."

"Why?"

"Because he got a girl in trouble and had to get married." The guy caught himself, and didn't say what he was about to say, but started laughing. "Do you know I have a little boy at home too? And what he likes to do better than anything is pepper me with questions. I am not playing the 'why' game, so you better ask something that's not a "why," and I'll answer, as long as it doesn't interfere with my work."

Mario examined the wire the other guy had poked through from the outside, and watched while the fat guy screwed a plastic thing on the wall and snipped the wire.

"Is that where the TV comes from?"

"That's just a wire from the antenna. We could just let you stick a hanger on the top of the TV but you don't have good reception here. The antenna has rods on it that act like ears, and they can hear the TV signal from the towers where it is broadcast to send the signal down the wire."

"When you cut the wire, why doesn't all the TV didn't pour out, like when the fire hydrant sprung a leak in the summer?"

Mario liked the idea of playing in shooting streams of color TV, the way they played in sprays of water in the summer.

The Dearden's guy laughed. "No way. The wire just carries electronic signals that have to be converted."

"Oh." Mario said, "Then does the electronic pour out?"

"No. And it's called electricity."

"Why not?" Mario slapped his hand over his mouth.

The guy scratched his head, and responded anyway.

"I don't know. You would have to ask an electrician."

"Where can I find a 'lectrician to ask?"

"You'll have to check the yellow pages."

Mario took a breath, about to ask another question, but the Dearden's guy put a finger over his lips and whispered, "Shhh."

He held up two wires and showed him a screwdriver.

"You have to sit very quietly because the components might blow up if there is talking while the wires are getting connected."

Mario got very quiet. He didn't believe the whole "blowing up" thing but had plenty of experience with people telling him to shut up.

***

From the living room, Mario couldn't quite see Hollenbeck Park where all the gang action was, but it was just a block away. The corner girls who worked 4th and Soto hung out in the park when they weren't on a date, but he couldn't see them from his window. He thought they looked like flowers, with their bright hair and colorful clothes. He'd wave at them when he saw them, and call them by name; and they'd call back, "Hey Mario," and call him big man. They'd moved their business away from the church, like the good Catholic girls they were. It was a big secret from the church ladies that Aunt Carmen knew them all. Sometimes the corner girls would bring babies to her to bring to the church. Aunt Carmen was always happy when she'd talked one of them into keeping her baby, but then she'd leave and Mario didn't see her any more.

He could see the constant traffic to and from the church next door, and St. Mary School for girls which was behind the church. Of course, he also saw the neighborhood kids playing on the sidewalk. There wasn't room to play in the tiny yard in front of the apartment building, and be-sides that, the landlord had a sixth sense. The minute anyone set foot on that mostly imaginary patch of grass, that fat old Hector ran out of his first floor apartment waving his broom like it was a sword and he was the last of the Conquistadors. He'd usually get one good wallop in on one of the slower kids like Tortuga. Then he'd straighten up the little "keep off the grass" sign, brush off his white wingtips, and go back inside. He wasn't all bad, though. Sometimes he would go to 4th and Soto and give the cor-ner girls money.

Theirs was a small apartment but when Mario got back from visiting his friends' places, it didn't seem so small. His friends' two bedrooms were packed full of brothers and sisters crammed into a single bedroom, taking turns on who slept in a sleeping bag, and who used the twin beds. With all of those people living practically on top of each other, neither were they squeaky clean. By contrast, Aunt Carmen was a meticulous house-keeper. Their tiny dining room table was always beautifully set, and if the carpeting smelled a little moldy sometimes, usually all you noticed was the delicious scent of her carne picada, or enchiladas baking in the oven. In their creaky, old refrigerator, there were always pinto beans, refried beans or beans refried in cheese, and Mexican rice, and tortillas. On days that she walked home from work, she stopped in the Mexican bakery, and brought back sweet Mexican bread, and once in a while a small cake. It was not a bad childhood. Sometimes he wished he could skip school like some of his friends and run parts for the neighborhood chop shops, or be a mule which sounded like fun, but Auntie Carmen would never let him. She said they didn't need the extra money, and he better stay in school because he wasn't all that smart, and needed everything a teacher could drum into him.

He waited for her arrival at home everyday. The bus stop was just two minutes from their apartment. As soon as she was home, she'd busy herself cooking dinner. She'd usually send him off to play until she called him in, when they would sit down together to eat. There were no exceptions to the routine. On weekends when she did not work, they walked to the market six blocks away and did the buying for the week at the Safeway on 1st Street. They carried the purchases in brown paper shopping bags that they emptied out when they got home, then folded them neatly so they could use them around the house.

Mario was a so-so student. His aunt expected him to be a genius and a saint. He was good at reading and spelling and could write a pretty good paper, but hated all the other subjects, including math. It's too bad they didn't teach Spanish at school because he was as good in Spanish as English. He grew up speaking both. His aunt always said that someday everybody's first language was going to be Spanish. He could never be a saint (or a genius for that matter) but he couldn't tell her that because he loved her too much. Plus, he hated homework. He also hated how his aunt turned off the television until he could prove he was done. He always dashed it off as fast as he could.

She cast a big shadow in the neighborhood. He didn't really understand it, but all of the neighborhood was in awe of her. It wasn't something he discussed with his friends, but it was obvious that no one respected the other moms the way everyone respected Aunt Carmen. No one went to the other moms for advice, or knocked on their doors at midnight when a baby was on the way. No matter the time of day or night, when they came for help, she was always there; but she was just Aunt Carmen to him. She was always there to help him too. He loved her, and often thought about calling her mom. He remembered when he was little, he called her Mami and Mamita, and he had called Moonie, Papi, but he was too big to do that now since he knew better.

He hated to think of what she'd do if she ever saw his friends and him hiding in the tiny backyard shared by other apartments when they were poring through the stash of men's magazines that, along with Carson's mother, sisters and Carson himself, had been abandoned by Carson's father. It was common for one of the boys to borrow one of the books, especially one with a centerfold, overnight. Mario was no exception. His curiosity about women was growing. One day, his friend Carson came over as he often did with one of the men's magazines. This one was a black and white issue with pictures of men and women, naked. Some of the pictures showed a man and woman having sex.

That was the day his Aunt heard him use the word "fuck."

"Carson," his auntie told his friend. "Go home."

It was bad enough when she gave Mario a horrendous lecture on language and respect, but when she caught him looking at the magazine which his friend had so casually left open on his bed, she found the end of her patience. She never spanked him, ever, but what she did that day was far worse, as far as he was concerned.

"This Sunday, you have to go down on your knees and work your way all the way to the altar."

He heard the decree in horror. He'd seen older boys who had all done it before when they had gotten caught lying, fighting or stealing candy from the bodega. It was embarrassing, and they got kidded about it for weeks afterward. It hadn't made them better people, either, just better at hiding what they did.

"Auntie, you can't do that to me, you can't!"

He cried. He begged. He protested in every possible way, and at every possible opportunity. It didn't do any good. His middle name might secretly be Sanchez, but Auntie's middle name was stubborn.

That following Sunday, just as the morning mass started, she made him do it.

He went down on his knees and worked his way all the way to the altar.

It was a long way. Row after row. He could hear people whispering and rustling in the pews he passed. He could feel their eyes on him. It had only seemed to be such a long way once before, and that was when he'd taken his first communion when he was eight. Back then, he'd told himself that after the big church ceremony, that would be all of it. Then he could be done with the church thing. But no, Aunt Carmen had him on his knees, again—still.

It was loco how this crawl down the aisle took forever, longer even than taking catechism for that whole year when he was seven. The only break he got was that he didn't have to go down the center aisle. Aunt Carmen saw there was an older boy in the middle, and had agreed to allow him to take a side aisle, but it was still so humiliating. The church was packed. The kids who saw him—Japanese kids on one side of the aisle, Mexican kids on the other—whispered and pointed and giggled, even Carson. At least the Jewish kids weren't there. Carson, who should have known better, giggled along with everyone else, but it was his father's magazines which were responsible; and the only thing standing between Carson and his own crawl of shame was Mario's sense of loyalty. The only person who ignored what he was doing was the priest.

Even his best friends hated him after that Sunday because his humiliation inspired a wave of penance fever in their mothers, who followed in his aunt's steps by making their children crawl in Mario's knee-steps. They'd all had to do it when they were kids, especially the ones from the Mexican side of the city, who told horror stories of how they had to do their penance starting outside on rocks two miles uphill all the way to the church. He envied the Japanese kids, who said they didn't do that back in Japan. He asked for God's help in keeping his aunt from catching him again with one of those magazines, or using four letter words. He didn't think God cared, but he knew Aunt Carmen couldn't handle it.

He came home from school one day to find the resident manager blocking the door of their apartment. Mario knew Hector pretty well. Sometimes he'd hire the older boys to use the push mower on the grass. Mario had asked to do it before, but he was always too young. He wondered what Hector was doing there.

Once Mario had been coming home from school and passed Señor Chapo harping at the landlord over the dried grass clippings all over, because his dogs would sneak bites of the grass when they were out on their daily walks, and then yack it up all over his clean floors. Old Hector always listened to Señor Chapo, when he didn't listen to anybody else, maybe because he always paid his rent, or maybe because he could have moved whenever he wanted, or maybe because he knew the guy who really owned the apartments. Señor Chapo only stayed because he didn't like change. But he didn't like his dog yacking up lawn clippings either.

"You, boy!" Señor Chapo had called him over.

It was strange to be called "boy" because they were such good friends. Señor Chapo was so sweet on Aunt Carmen that he let her win at poker, bought her big boxes of candy and flowers, and called Mario "Mister Luna." Being called "boy" was out of the ordinary.

Mario pointed to himself, and said, "Me?"

"Yes, you."

So Mario joined them.

Señor Chapo shoved a push broom at him. Its handle was easily six feet long, and the brush on the bottom was roughly half that.

"Sweep up this grass, boy," he said, giving Mario a secret wink, and pointing at the walk stretching end to end in front of the apartments. Mario, who was accustomed to Carmen getting him to do chores like this, raced through it, no big deal since it was a straight shot, and there was no sofa to move. He had a good sized pile when he was done, pushed it right up to the trash can and scooped it in using the rusted "APARTMENT TO LET" sign like a shovel. He was glad Carson wasn't around because he liked nothing better than to screech GERONIMO and leap into leaves and lawn clippings so that they scattered everywhere. He'd also want a cut of the profits, if there were any to be had, even if he'd done nothing to earn it. Mario brought the broom back, and Señor Chapo bullied Hector into tossing Mario all his pocket change for doing the job. After that, Hector was good for lunch money on the days he paid bigger boys to mow. Once, Carson had dumped clippings on the walk and asked for the sweeping job. Hector had seen him do it, yelled at him to get lost, and paid Mario a half dollar to clean it up.

But today was not lawn day. The walk was swept already. It wasn't even the first of the month. So why was Hector standing in the door to the apartment?

Mario was about to barge right in, but some cunning instinct made him hold back and eavesdrop. He only heard bits and pieces. Auntie was speaking in English, saying something about "no more overtime at work—cutting hours," "management changes," and "being put on payroll" and something everyone was always complaining about, "taxes." He didn't understand all of it and only grasped the significance at the end, when his aunt said clearly, "Let me know when a one bedroom becomes available."

That was a shock. A one bedroom apartment meant that he would not have his own room. He had always had his own room, as far back as he could remember. He thought in horror of having to share a bedroom with his aunt the way his friends shared their rooms, taking turns with the bed and the sleeping bag on the floor.

To Mario's great relief, fat old Hector was shaking his head. But Aunt Carmen looked like she was about to cry. He was saying that unless someone had some kind of emergency, nothing would be opening up in the next couple months except one of the bigger, more expensive corner apartments with the side porch and separate dining room.

"Of course I could come in, and we could talk about it," Hector said.

"No."

"I can be nice," Hector said.

"I am not that desperate, and you are not that lucky."

"We can go out for a drink."

"The amount of alcohol I would need to drink to sleep with you would actually kill me."

That didn't sound at all like Aunt Carmen, but Mario figured he'd misunderstood. A few seconds later, the door slammed so hard it bounced back open. Hector, who stood there unmoving for a few minutes, had the good sense not to push the door to go inside, and walked off muttering something under his breath. Mario came out from behind the pillar. His aunt was so distracted she didn't even see him walk through the open door.

"What did the landlord want?"

"To be a jerk."

Carmen was hunched over the dinette scribbling on a piece of scrap paper, writing figures and crossing them out until she finally wadded it up and tossed it in the trash. Mario slipped past her and went into his own room, shutting the door.

He gazed around. He didn't have much. His single twin bed with its faded cover and the extra blanket folded neatly at the foot. The end table with its thrift store lamp and the wind-up alarm clock that woke him in time for school every morning. His very own closet, in which hung a few changes of clothes he was constantly outgrowing, a shelf above the pole, and a box on the floor for things he called his own. This space, his space, even the squeaky old door, was suddenly very precious to him. The situation was urgent.

Plus the apartment had a secret. All the other apartments vented to the roof. Because of the wiring in this one unit, the stove was against the neighbor's wall, so the vent had to make a turn.

Long before they'd moved in, an upstairs neighbor had gone out of town, and left the bathtub stopper in. The leaky bath tub faucet had dripped for four days, quietly filling and overflowing until the ceiling downstairs had fallen in. Instead of hiring a professional, Hector himself had done the repairs. The results were about what you'd expect, with the off and on switches in the kitchen being reversed. Aunt Carmen had once speculated that maybe the electrician who did this apartment was drunk on the job, or maybe he wired it on a Monday morning, after tying one on, prompting Hector to admit that was not the case. He knew, because he'd performed the repairs himself!

One consequence of the repairs is that instead of emerging on the roof, the stove exhaust pipe intersected with the section of ductwork from the bathroom, and came out exactly where Aunt Carmen had put the couch against the wall. That vent was Mario's secret weapon. He didn't have to stress over secrets grownups kept. If they were going to talk trash, and send him out of the room, he could go into the kitchen and hear it all. Since the vent system was hooked up to the bathroom fan, he could hear couch conversation in the bathroom (and vice versa, which is why he knew Aunt Carmen's singing was never going to land her on *The Ed Sullivan Show*.) He could hear even if he was sent outside, as long as he stood by the right spot by the fan's output. Where would he get another apartment where he could eavesdrop on the grownups?

He had to do something to keep them from having to move to a smaller apartment. He needed to get a job. He looked at himself in the mirror. He was one of the tallest kids at school, skinny. He wondered what he'd have to do to look older to get a job. He only had one skill that he knew of—the gift of gab. He could talk a mile a minute, and it constantly got him in trouble. The same mouth was always talking him out of trouble, too. But was that something he could get paid for?

The possibility of losing their place was probably the biggest shock of his life since he had met Pélon.

When he was a little kid, his aunt had been working all day, as she always had, and he stayed during the day with a neighbor who had a bunch of daughters and a talkative little son, Carson, his own age. Carson's dad went out one night and never came back. Carson's mom had gone to work, and both Carson and Mario had started staying with Pélon's mom. The first big shock of his life had been Pélon, who was like a hurricane or earthquake or some other lunatic force of nature. Until they were six and started first grade, it had been like having two brothers—quiet Carson and crazy Pélon—one aunt, and two moms. Carson and Pélon had been very different though. Carson, who was soft-spoken and a little whiney, had been very grateful to hang around a boy his own age, especially coming from a houseful of older sisters who managed to cater to his every wish, at the same time they bossed him around at every turn.

Pélon was different from the beginning. Pélon, by the way, wasn't really his name. No one even remembered his name. Everybody called him Pélon. Pelón means baldy. And he wasn't even a baldy; he had a full head of hair. It was always slicked back with pomade. He was a true, true gang-banger before there was the name for one. Once they had been the same size, but now that they were ten, Mario was twice Pélon's height. But if Mario had twice the height, Pélon had four times the meanness. Pélon was king, even back before he was six. He might have shared his mother with five brothers plus Carson and Mario, but there was no question at Pélon's house who was boss. After that first day at Pélon's, Carson got even quieter. Sometimes Mario wondered what Pélon had done that got Carson to turn so quiet, but he never asked. Aunt Carmen got a funny look in her eye when he talked to her about it.

"Never mind," she assured Mario, "I have a gut feeling no one will ever be taking advantage of you that way. For you, Pélon is a bully, like Señor Chapo's Chihuahua is scrappy to his Great Dane. You're going to be big, like the Great Dane, so you must never be a bully, even if your nature tells you to."

Mario thought it better not to tell Pélon that Aunt Carmen had compared him to Ella.

Señor Chapo and his two mismatched dogs lived on the other side of the thin wall. Mario knew them well. Ella Grande, a long haired Chihuahua, reigned, every inch a jaunty princess, from her perked ears and razor teeth to the trimmed ends of her silky coat. The crisp contrast of black coat to snowy tuxedo always caught Mario's eye, who saw in Ella the society woman in long white gloves emerging from a limo on the way to the opera—a still he'd seen in the society section of the LA Times, snapped by a photographer. No image could do justice to her cocky walk, or her crazy, Jekyll and Hyde disassociation when overcome by instant shrill fits of rage, barking, snarling and biting furiously when disturbed by some outside sound, or when anyone approached her beloved señor. She loved Pélon, hated Carson, and though she only tolerated Mario, whenever she sneaked out of the apartment, Señor Chapo sent Mario out to get her. He was the only one she would come to.

Perhaps Ella's devilish and queenly attitude was entirely her own; or perhaps it was exacerbated by her entourage of one, the Harlequin Great Dane known as Hermanito, the size of a Shetland pony, mild as milk, who never snuck out, and rarely barked. When he did, the whole building trembled. He was big, even for a Great Dane. Like Ella, his ears and tail were uncut. Where Ella had a long, sleek black coat, Hermanito's fur was short and white with a couple of splotches as if someone had hit him a couple of times with an ink-dipped dodge ball. One summer when there was nothing to do, a black circle appeared spontaneously around one of Hermanito's placid brown eyes, sparking the rumor that Hermanito had run away and been replaced with another dog. Mario knew that wasn't true. First, he knew Hermanito, and Hermanito knew him. Second, it was no accident that new mark looked just like the one on Petey, the dog on the Little Rascals reruns. After the pirate patch dye job eventually rubbed off, the general consensus had laid the blame on Pélon. Mario said nothing publicly. He was no rat. But privately he assured Pélon that he knew he hadn't dyed Hermanito. If Pélon had done it, the circle would have been red. Mario had his own opinion who was responsible, but he kept those thoughts to himself.

Before they were five years old, the boys would hang around on Friday, waiting for the working mothers to come home with their pay. Friday was poker night, a big event when the moms would converge around the rickety table in Pélon's mom's chaotic kitchen, drink beer, and eat botanas and salted plums. Sometimes Señor Chapo or other neighbors sat in. For Pélon's mom, it was the reason she was babysitting; she needed the income, especially when she was between boyfriends. For Carson's mom with a factory job, the game was a chance to complain to an understanding audience about her low wages and high taxes. As for Aunt Carmen, she talked about how thankful she was to be paid cash, that even though she was paid less, she brought home more. Her fifty dollars a week seemed a fortune to Mario. Five of it went to Pélon's mom, sometimes paid in six packs of her favorite beer, which Pélon's mom preferred. No one tried too hard to win, because the big winner always had to provide next week's first case of Corona.

The week after they almost lost their apartment, after school every day Mario raced to Brooklyn Avenue, and walked from one end to the other, contemplating asking for a job. The more he walked, the more bashful he got. He was too shy to walk in cold, though he'd been running errands on his own in the neighborhood since he could lisp his own name and reach a door knob.

Finally, he turned off Brooklyn and walked a block to the Italian restaurant. The door swung open, and delicious air wafted over him, redolent of roasting tomatoes, and spices, and hot garlic bread. It made his stomach growl.

Mario walked up to the counter, where a black-haired girl was engrossed in a flirtation with a man with a bin of dirty dishes and peach fuzz on his chin. Mario thumped the counter to get her attention, and then it still took a minute for her to notice him.

"Yeah kid? You lost?" She grinned. "You getting a pizza or something? Pony up."

Mario didn't know about ponies so he just told her, "I need a job."

"You better ask the boss, Uncle Nicky," she said, pointing to a small group. "He's the grouchy one. Good luck kid. You'll need it."

The guy with the bin of dishes snatched a coin off a table and tossed it to him.

"For luck," he said. "You'll need it if you're gonna talk to Uncle Nicky," but Mario could tell he'd done it to irritate the waitress, who started in on the dishwasher about snatching her tips. Mario held out the coin to the waitress, who flushed, and told him to keep it, as Mario had known she would, but she kept sniping at the dish man.

Mario made a beeline for the man she'd pointed out as Uncle Nicky, sitting amongst a bunch of men who looked just like him, all crowded around a long table with a red-checked tablecloth, all wearing spaghetti stained white shirts and pants, all forking spaghetti into their mouths like they were in a race, and shoveling it in with chunks of bread from a big basket. One of them was wearing a suit.

"Are you Uncle Nicky?"

Mario waited to be acknowledged, but the guy never looked up. The restaurant was a clatter of voices and dishware, the yelling match between the busboy and the waitress, kitchen pots and pans clanging, a tinny chorus of silverware against china, the scraping of chairs on the hardwood floor, and the horns of cars stuck in traffic outside. Somewhere, a phone rang, and an unseen woman said, "Will that be here or to go?"

Mario took a deep breath, and yelled at the top of his lungs, "Uncle Nicky!"

All eating at the table stopped, and all the men stared at him.

Uncle Nicky stopped in mid-chew with a startled look at Mario. He squinted, and leaned over, peering closely at Mario's face. He shrugged, belched, and expertly waved around a massive spool of spaghetti on his fork without it unraveling. Mario watched the wiggling noodle with some fascination, waiting for it to fall, but it never did.

"Sit down kid, and have some spaghetti."

Mario didn't wait for a second invitation. Aunt Carmen always said he ate like he had a tapeworm. He could have a dinner at Pélon's, at Carson's, and polish off a third one at Aunt Carmen's table, and no one ever the wiser. He sat down, and inhaled the pasta from a plate that was shoved in front of him, mimicking the efficient twirl-and-shovel style of the men at the table. They burped, and he burped too, though his was less impressive.

They all laughed.

"Break's over," Nicky said. Mario had never seen so many big men move so fast. In seconds, the table cleared, except for a guy in a suit, Mario, and Uncle Nicky.

"Uncle Nicky, I need a job."

"Which one of my prolific sisters is your ma, kid? I don't seem to recall your name."

"Must be one of your sisters' kids." The guy in the suit pointed at Mario with a fork loaded with pasta. "You ain't ugly enough to be one of Nardo's. They all look like they was smashed in the face with a trash can lid."

Nicky laughed and said, "Guess I can always use another nephew who can wash dishes."

"I live with Aunt Carmen," Mario volunteered.

"I don't have a sister named Carmen," Nicky said, frowning. "Say, what kind of a fast one are you trying to pull?"

"I'm trying to get a job."

"Who do you think I am?"

"You're Uncle Nicky," Mario pointed at the counter girl. "She said."

Nicky glared in the direction of the girl who was hiding behind a magazine, and flung a mouthful of Italian in her direction before he turned back to Mario.

"Do I look like the help-wanted section of the Los Angeles Times? Do you see me wearing a help-wanted sign, hiring any bum off the street? You do not. I can't keep my worthless family employed, much less strangers."

Like the crowd who had left the table, Nicky was wearing a red spattered apron, white shirt and pants. He needed a shave. Crumbs and part of a meatball were on the tablecloth. Aunt Carmen would have slapped his hand, and made him clean off the table before he took another bite.

"I am not one of your worthless family," Mario said. "She said you were the boss, Uncle Nicky." Mario pointed again toward the girl hostess, who quickly turned away, but was still behind the counter, chewing gum and reading from a movie magazine, and pretending she wasn't eavesdropping.

"I don't need no more help."

"I can do dishes."

"I'm thinking about firing her for letting you in here," Uncle Nicky said. "I'd fire her for sure if she wasn't my sister's kid."

Mario sat behind his empty plate, wondering if he could ask for seconds.

Uncle Nicky stood up.

So did Mario.

"Beat it," Nicky yelled, launching a football of hard bread at his head. Mario caught the loaf before it smacked him.

"Thanks," he said. "Aunt Carmen's spaghetti is better than yours."

Uncle Nicky's face turned scarlet.

"Hey kid," the girl hostess put down her magazine and yelled, "He didn't mean that as a gift. Better get lost before he charges you. And when I say get lost, I mean run like hell."

Suddenly, everyone was yelling in Italian. Nicky made a grab for Mario who dodged and made for the door. So did Uncle Nicky. Mario ran through a gauntlet of what he guessed was Italian profanity, hit the door at full speed, and hot-footed it all the way back to Brooklyn Avenue. When Uncle Nicky didn't follow, Mario sat down on Brooklyn on the curb, and leaning against a building where he had a good view of the door of the Italian restaurant and the rest of the street, munched the butter-soaked garlicy bread he'd caught in mid air, and watched people go by.

"Uncle Nicky's not so tough," Mario said. "If that's the worst that could happen. And I got lunch out of the deal." He wiped off the crumbs and looked for "Help Wanted" signs. There still weren't any, but the lack of a sign still didn't stop him from opening each door he passed, and going in to ask for a job. Each time he'd start, his gift of gab would desert him, leaving him frozen and embarrassed, mumbling something unintelligible to the clerk, and then he'd walk out a penny poorer with a piece of candy. His pockets filled up. He was lucky the busboy had tossed him a quarter and not a nickel.

Squeezed between two restaurants was a familiar sight, the karate and judo school with the red-painted alley behind it. All week, each time Mario passed by, the little man inside seemed to be watching him. He wondered if the old guy was going to call the cops about the graffiti wall. He got nervous and took the long way around the block to get home.

Somewhere in the neighborhood, a police siren or an ambulance blared, getting louder instead of quieter, and a woman with a good set of lungs was yelling every few minutes, and fading off, but otherwise, things were pretty quiet. Carson looked behind him but didn't see any flashing lights, so he continued up the walk to Mario's house. He wasn't the first one there. Pélon had nabbed a softball from somewhere and was bouncing it into the Lunas' door, and catching it before it hit the ground. Every time he did it, Ella Grande next door would go into a shrill barking frenzy, along with an upstairs neighbor who screamed out the window for him to cut it out.

"You ready, Miss Big?" Pélon asked softly, winding up. Behind her door, Ella Grande, AKA Miss Big, whined.

"Where's Mario?" Carson asked. "I haven't seen him all afternoon."

"Beats me."

Pélon took a step back, did another wind up like the big D, Don Drysdale. The ball hit the door hard, inspiring Ella to tune up again, and bounced at an angle, before it flew off into the dirt where Carson grabbed it. This made Pélon swear, because Carson would never throw it back like a normal guy, only hold it out of reach, taunting him till he went apeshit. Today was no exception.

"Bet you can't get it," Carson said.

Pélon tossed his hand-me-down glove and launched himself into Carson's midsection. They rolled around on the ground for a few minutes before Pélon got the ball back. Carson was somewhat the worse for wear. Pélon never pulled his punches.

Unfazed, Carson said, "I passed Aunt Carmen on the way here. She hadn't seen Mario either. He missed a trip to the bakery, and that's not like him."

"Speak of the Devil," Pélon said, and they both watched as Aunt Carmen rounded the corner. Right behind her, a police car screeched to a halt, siren still squealing. Aunt Carmen didn't slow her brisk pace, not until the cop jumped out of the car and blocked her way.

"Look, it's Dibble."

Dibble was a recent nickname for the beat cop, a young officer born and raised in LA but close enough to his Latin roots that he seemed more like one of the neighborhood guys playing dress-up than a real cop. No one knew his real name. He'd taken a fancy to the nickname stolen from *Top Cat*. Dibble was on his nameplate.

The boys were too far to hear what was being said even if the siren wasn't drowning out everything else, but they ran closer. Their mothers were sure to ask for details, so they waited to see Aunt Carmen hauled off, as so many people were.

Dibble hadn't yet shoved her up against his car, or handcuffed her; he was waving his hands around, talking and pointing toward the apartment building. She shook her head in response to something he said. Then the cop pointed right at them.

Carmen turned around and looked in their direction.

"Carson! Pélon!"

"Shit," Pélon said, looking nervous. He had too many big brothers who got into too much trouble too often not to have misgivings about running toward an officer of the law, even if it was a guy who had taken the time on his day off to put up a basketball goal in the parking lot. "Why'd she have to say my name out loud to the cop? I gotta go." He snatched his glove and ball and ran for home.

Carson approached with some misgiving and his best manners.

"Hello, Mrs. Luna."

Carmen's eyebrows raised at the unaccustomed formality. "Carson, have you seen Mario?" raising her voice over the noise of the siren. "Could you turn that down?" she asked the cop.

Carson's mouth fell open when the cop did what she asked and turned off the siren. He came closer.

"Have you seen Mario?"

Carson shook his head. "No ma'am. Not since school let out."

"When you see him, tell him that Margarita's baby is on the way. He knows what to do. Most likely, I won't be home till morning. He'll have to stay at your house or Pélon's."

She glanced toward the officer. "I usually give Mario more notice, and have somewhere for him to go when it is time, but this one is an early bird." She turned back toward Carson, "Do you understand what to tell Mario?"

Carson nodded.

She started to walk.

Dibble glanced at his watch, and pointed to the back side of the apartment building.

"It will be faster in the cruiser with the grocery bags and all."

"It's just around the corner."

Dibble said, "Let me help."

Carmen nodded, relenting. The cop opened the door to the cruiser's back seat, relieved her of the grocery bags and put them in, then opened the front passenger side and held the door open for Carmen, a thing Carson had only seen in the movies. While Carson watched open-mouthed, the cop shut the doors, ran around to the driver's side, and got in, just like a limo driver. The siren wailed to life as the car rocketed to the backside of the building, and screeched to a stop.

Carson ran to Mario's house and pocketed the key from under the mat, then veered right, took the shortcut through his own house, slamming through the kitchen, and passing through the crowd of his sisters to dash out the back door, where he made it just in time to see Carmen hurry into the apartment where the woman had been screaming all day.

Carson dashed off to Pélon's and found him surrounded by neighbors who had been drawn outside by the sound of the siren but who had emerged too late to see anything. They had converged near the basketball goal. Carson had no desire deliver his message and then have to share his bed with Mario which is what would happen if Mario slept over. Carson had a bed-wetting issue that he didn't want to become public knowledge. Besides, their apartment was already too crowded.

"The cops just took Aunt Carmen away!" Carson said, conveniently leaving out the part about the cop dropping her off around back, carrying in the groceries for her, and Mario needing a place to spend the night.

Before anyone started asking questions, he added, "I gotta find Mario."

"I think I can find him," Pélon said, horrified to hear that Carmen had been arrested.

"Well, you boys do it, then," Pélon's mother said.

Carson understood that as code for the grown-ups wanting them to beat it so they could gossip. He heard a door slam, and saw his mother coming to join the clique, so he ducked out of the huddle to hit the sidewalk with Pélon.

"Where are you looking for him?"

Pélon gestured toward Brooklyn.

"I'll look the other direction," Carson volunteered. "By school, I guess."

They parted ways.

Discouraged, Mario was making his way home when he ran into Pélon.

"I don't know what a man's gotta do to find a job," Mario said. "But I been looking."

Pélon looked shocked. In all his ten years, getting a job had never occurred to him.

"Why?"

Mario looked cagey. "It's not like we need the money or anything," he said.

"Maybe you do," Pélon said. "The cops took your aunt away."

"They what?" Mario asked, dumbfounded. "I don't think I heard you right."

"You just gotta get a job, Mario," Pélon said wisely, "for bail or ransom or whatever they call it, because Carson saw the cops take your Aunt Carmen away. When the cops take someone, it always takes money to get them back."

"You're right," Mario said heavily. "It's up to me. I guess I better head up there, and see how much I gotta have to get her out of the clink."

"Maybe you gotta have the money first." Pélon said. "Will they even talk to you if you're broke?"

"I don't know," Mario said. "I guess I better get a job first."

He made a mad dash back to his house, Pélon at his heels, but when he looked under the mat, the house key was gone.

"Maybe it got kicked off the sidewalk," Pélon suggested, feeling guiltier by the second. "I was playing ball here earlier. Maybe I kicked it off somewhere."

A door slammed close by. One of his brothers called Pélon's name. The boys held their breath till they heard the door shut.

"Coast is clear."

They searched the garden, the sidewalk, and the mat again. They looked for fifteen minutes, finding nothing but dirt before they sat on the curb to consider what to do next. It was getting dark.

"Surely you're not 'victed already," Pélon said. "Every time we get 'victed, the resident manager beats on the door every day for a week, then they haul our stuff to the curb, then they put a sign on the door, and Mama has to borrow money from your auntie to get back in." He wiped off the window with his elbow and peeked inside. "You still got all your stuff."

"But it's in there, and I'm out here." Mario thought about seeing the landlord in his house the week before. "I don't know."

"Come home with me," Pélon said. "You can have dinner, and dig up a sleeping bag, and we can figure out what to do next."

Mario thought about it, but shook his head. This wasn't the usual. When a baby came, Aunt Carmen was just out for the night, and she always made plans for him with one of the moms in the neighborhood. This was a for-real crisis. Aunt Carmen was too proud to accept charity so he would have to be too. Mario couldn't show up somewhere with his hand out, and start the gossip up.

"Hey, Pélon!" It was the voice of a different brother.

"I'm coming, don't bust a gut!" Pélon yelled back. "I gotta go in," he said softly. "You gonna be ok? Maybe I should stay out here with you."

"I'm good," Mario lied.

He watched Pélon go inside. He tried the door of his apartment again. It was still locked.

He had been out at night before, but only in his own yard, surrounded by family. Off Brooklyn, with the night traffic whizzing by, the character of the neighborhood changed when the sun went down, into a landscape both familiar and alien. The night was cool, the air heavy with the odor of traffic and restaurants. Mario's stomach growled, confused by bus fumes, tormented by delicious odors wafting from the Jewish Deli, the Chinese, Italian and Mexican restaurants that were all still open after dark. He hadn't yet actually missed a meal. He fished a piece of taffy from his pocket and shoved it in his mouth.

The police precinct was a washout. After walking seven long blocks from Hollenbeck Park, he asked the desk sergeant for Aunt Carmen, but they'd misunderstood, and on the loudspeaker, asked Carmen Luna to the desk to claim her lost child. They sat him in a chair beside a bowl of jelly beans, which he emptied into his pocket. They were all rushing around doing different things so it was easy to slip out. He followed the sidewalk thoughtlessly, finding himself at the entrance to the alley that had been the canvas for Pélon's can of spray paint. Invisible cars drove down Brooklyn, blinding him with their lights. He ducked into the alley. Three brick walls surrounded him and made an L shaped space behind the oriental studio. He turned left, and saw there was a new light up, a bare bulb by the studio's back door. Maybe the old guy had put it up to keep them from spraying the wall again, but Mario was glad of it. The illumination made the corner seem almost homey and familiar. The clubhouse looked almost as welcoming as his room at home. Of course there were no pillows or sheets, but the cushions were as good as a bed.

Mario lifted the door and crawled in. It was so dark inside that a minute later he propped the door up. It wasn't tall enough for him to stand, but it was easily long enough to stretch out. He rested his head up by the opening, polished off the old bag of popcorn and the rest of his candy, and fell right to sleep. The next thing he knew, the sun was up. He stretched and reached for the blanket, but there wasn't one. The mattress was scratchy, his back itched, and his room smelled funny. He was fully dressed, even to his shoes.

"What's for breakfast, Auntie? I'm starving," he yelled, but the strange reverberating tone of his voice brought him to the sense of something wrong.

He rubbed his eyes, and sat up to get his bearings. It all came back in a rush: Aunt Carmen arrested. Needing a job. Locked out of his house. He stashed the broom handle, and closed the clubhouse. He supposed he'd have to go to school, as if it was a normal day.

Normal. The alien landscape was gone. Back to the familiar brick-walled alley. The old guy had been out. The wall was wet where he had scrubbed away some but not all of the paint. He must have just done it too; there was a standing puddle of something that smelled like turpentine, and a scrub brush. Mario felt lucky the guy hadn't seen him there, asleep in the box, or he'd have called the cops.

Without thinking, Mario grabbed the brush and went to town like Ella Grande digging on her favorite hole to China. The blistered paint was gunky, and though it came off easily, underneath was a red stain.

The quality of light felt like early morning. He thought again about school. He'd better go. Mario wiped his hands off on his pants and smoothed his hair, but had no idea of the time. He came out of the alley. He couldn't see in, but rubbed the window of the shop with his elbow, and cupped his hands against the glass to see if he could make out the clock inside. It took him a few seconds to register that he was face to face with the old guy inside, who was calmly drinking a cup of tea and staring back.

Mario shrieked, and fell back on his ass.

The door to the shop opened.

"Yes?" the old guy said.

At least there was no trace of red paint on his face. Good. Maybe the geezer had forgotten about it. He took a sip of tea from a delicate looking blue and white tea cup with no handle.

Mario mumbled something.

"What?"

"I was trying to see the clock, to tell if I'm late for school."

"You go to school?"

"Of course I go to school. Everybody goes to school." Mario guessed that maybe the man really had forgotten about who painted the wall. Or maybe he hadn't gotten a good look at Pélon and him the other day. He gathered his confidence. "Hey man, my name is Mario, I'm looking for a job after school."

"I'm Cosmo. I'm going to be looking for a job too if I don't get some business in here. I should be out there on the West side. No one here wants to get into karate or judo."

"So you're selling karate and judo."

"Lessons."

The old man dipped the edge of a plain doughnut in his cup of tea. Mario's eyes followed the gesture, watched each dunk and nibble till only crumbs were left and then he watched as Cosmo ate those, too. Mario couldn't help it. He stared, and barely managed not to lick his lips. Mario's morning stomach was used to scarfing down a huge breakfast. His mouth watered, and he swallowed, reflexively. No pastry had ever looked so delicious. Cosmo opened the door wider, kicked the stop in place, and held out a doughnut.

"I got too many. If you don't eat them, I'll have to throw them away."

Mario looked at the doughnut. His stomach growled loud enough for the people across the street to hear.

"Don't mind if I do," he said. He wolfed one down. He could have eaten a dozen just like it. While he was eating, he looked down, and realized Cosmo had put the whole box on the sidewalk.

"Have all you want," Cosmo said. "They're day old. The whole box was just a penny."

Mario didn't hesitate. He grabbed another.

"You're younger than you look," Cosmo said. "Once you start talking, I can tell."

"I'm ten!"

"You're tall for your age," Cosmo observed, standing eye to eye. "You'd be perfect for karate. Maybe your mom and dad will get you lessons."

"There's three problems," Mario said. "I don't have any money for lessons, and you're not going to be here long enough to teach me anything.

You're moving to the West Side. And I don't have a mom and dad."

"No parents?"

"I live with Aunt Carmen," Mario said, his mouth full of a third doughnut. "She's better than parents." At least, she's better than parents when she was around, though he didn't say that aloud. He looked longingly at a fourth doughnut. "She'd probably make me stop at one doughnut though."

"A growing boy shouldn't be hungry," Cosmo said.

"I'm always hungry. And I'm looking for a job."

Traffic rumbled by on the street, and Mario remembered school again. He tried looking in the window but couldn't see the clock.

"Did you have the time?"

"Almost eight."

"I better run," Mario said. "I walk to school with the guys. Are you moving before this afternoon, or will you still be here?"

"I'm always here," Cosmo assured him.

"I'll be back at four," Mario said.

Class was the same as usual, except that Mario mooched lunch from everybody. He had a penny for a carton of milk, and got an apple and a banana from Carson who never ate fruit or vegetables, and half a peanut butter sandwich from Pélon.

Carson dug around his bag and gave him a squashed package of potato chips. "I'm not hungry," he said, burping. "I ate too much at dinner last night."

Mario noticed while he was eating that some of the girls were laughing behind their hands, and pointing at him.

"What's up with them?"

"Your shirt," Carson said.

Mario looked down. Yesterday's white shirt had gone several shades of gray, and was spotted with spaghetti grease, turpentine, red paint, and mystery dirt that must have been on the clubhouse cushions.

"Did you get a job yet?" Pélon asked.

"Not yet."

"Job?" Carson asked.

Mario didn't want to talk about his aunt at school, and didn't answer the question. He was worried about where she was.

"Let's meet at my place," Pélon said. Carson and Mario agreed.

"I can't stay long though, I gotta see a guy," Mario said.

Pélon loaned him a crowbar from his brother's toolbox, and Mario went home to try to jimmy his window. Just out of habit, first he checked under the mat, and lo and behold, the key was where it always was.

"Look," Mario said, holding it up for Pélon and Carson to see.

"It's back?" Pélon scratched his head and looked confused.

"So?" Carson said. "What do you mean, it's back?"

They didn't explain.

Mario opened the door.

Aunt Carmen was not there, but someone had made himself at home in the worst way possible. Dirty dishes were stacked and dumped out on the table and in the sink, crumbs, food and garbage covering every horizontal surface. The ceiling fan was slowly spinning with one of Mario's socks draped over a blade. The TV was on with the sound off, and the radio was on with the sound on. Sofa cushions were everywhere except actually on the sofa. The door to the fridge was standing open. The damage seemed to be confined to the kitchen and front room.

Pélon froze in the door, taken aback. "Wow. That's even worse than my house."

"You're gonna die," Carson said.

Mario pulled off his dirty shirt, balled it up and tossed it into the hamper.

"Don't just stand there," Mario said. "Clean something."

At the hint of work to be done, Carson and Pélon scattered like feral cats. Mario swept, mopped, washed, dried and put stuff away even faster than he'd done the day Aunt Carmen spotted the priest coming up the walk collecting for the Orphan Fund. He polished the floor half dry with his dirty clothes underfoot before he hit the shower, and threw on his Sunday best. He didn't want to be late to see Cosmo. Before he left, he cut a string of Aunt Carmen's leftover yarn and tied the key around his neck under his shirt. He wasn't getting locked out twice.

"Are you sure you're only ten?" Cosmo laughed and lit up a cigarette. "The only thing missing is the briefcase."

Mario had showed up wearing clean clothes, a too-big tie, a too-small jacket, and hair still wet from the shower.

Cosmo waved at people passing by, a fast walker, a couple of slow walkers, and a window shopper. Brooklyn Avenue was a busy street. "I was kidding this morning. I can't move. I have a lease. I'm stuck here."

Mario said, "Maybe I can get you some students."

Cosmo looked at him eye to eye as if Mario were a real grown-up.

"You do that, and I'll look real hard for a job for you."

Mario looked at the shop as if he'd never seen it before. And maybe he never had, not really. He noticed it now. Cosmo's studio was squeezed between two store fronts and the alley. On the alley side was a Mexican restaurant. On the other was a secondhand store where you could buy anything and everything. It was faced by two large glass windows with the name painted on one side, Brooklyn Avenue Karate/Judo, Learn Self-Defense. The other window had his name, Cosmo Hashimoto.

The door was in the middle.

The space the shop occupied was about 30 feet wide and 125 feet deep with an old bathroom in the back. Mario knew the size because down the street, there was one just like it to let, with the dimensions on the sign in magic marker, at least until Pélon had gotten his hands on that can of paint. Cosmo's office was a desk in one corner of the open space. To the front of the studio were mats. If a class was not going on, and it rarely was, they were rolled up. The hardwood floors were battered but so shiny they looked wet, even through the dusty storefront glass. It was so bare that at least once a week, someone from outside the neighborhood knocked on the window and stopped in to see if they could rent it. Against the wall were benches for the class to sit on, and two walls were mirrored.

"I'll see what I can do," Mario said.

They shook on it.

Chapter 2
Working Man

All the way home, Mario's mind was a storm cloud, turbulent with ideas and emotion. His head raced with possibilities with Cosmo. He could talk some kids into judo and karate, he felt sure. And then he'd have money, and then they wouldn't have to move. But then he'd have a flash of terror and remember Carmen in jail. He had been discouraged by the attitudes of the adults at the police station. They had shied him on. He could not make any of them understand he was looking for his aunt, not the other way around. At least when he was at the precinct, he'd had enough presence of mind to keep it cool. He'd had plenty experience witnessing bad consequences when there was a household with one parent who disappeared, and he didn't want that curse to hit his own household. Whether it was Big Juan, or Carson and his sisters, or Pélon and his brothers, the mother would disappear with a cop, and if none of them were old enough, the kids would disappear with Social Services. And it was sometimes weeks and weeks before things got back to normal, if ever. There had to be something he could pull so he would be okay on his own till his aunt got out. As long as he was free, he could always get her out. Based on what Pélon's brothers always had to say, he pictured Social Services as jail for kids, and to be avoided at any cost.

Maybe he could get one of Pélon's oldest brothers to go down with him; but that wouldn't do. He didn't trust them not to do the talking. They'd want to take charge, and they'd just screw things up.

He was preoccupied as he came up the walk, but not so preoccupied that he missed Hector trying to hammer the "KEEP OFF THE GRASS" sign so it would stand up.

Mario needed some cash. Carmen had already told Hector of the money pinch, so it couldn't hurt to ask.

"Do you need me do the walk?"

"Not today. You don't see no mower out, do you?"

"Oh," Mario said, thinking. "Take out your garbage?"

"No," Hector said decisively.

"Oh, ok," Mario sighed.

Hector looked pensive, and scratched his chin.

"I'll give you a quarter to get the bird crap off the Chevy's windshield."

Mario perked up. His years of watching Carmen haggling with food vendors kicked in. He got the ante up to fifty cents to do the whole car.

Even if he was soapy and dirty, he was whistling and feeling rich when he was done. Fifty cents was enough that he was able to come home with a day old loaf of that bread Aunt Carmen liked from the Mexican bakery, and still have a generous jingle in his pocket. He looked under the mat for his key before he recalled it was around his neck. At least he could get in and straighten up some more, and then he'd have to sit down and think about replenishing the rest of the groceries, because whoever had trashed their place had cleared out most everything that was already cooked.

He unlocked the door, and it creaked open as he dropped the key back around his neck. If things had been normal, Aunt Carmen would have had dinner on the stove by now. He put the bread on the dinette, and then did a little double take. When he left, he hadn't set the table for dinner, but there it was, set with plates and napkins and glasses. A couple of pots of something that smelled good were simmering on the stove.

And there she was—Aunt Carmen, big as life, asleep on the couch. At home, asleep, and not arrested! What did it mean? Mario was excited and relieved and curious all at once. He wasn't going to have to fend off social services after all. She wasn't wearing the striped prison uniform they always had in the movies.

The jacket she always wore to the office was draped over a chair, and her high heeled pumps were where she had kicked them off. He carried them to her room, and shoved them under the bed where she usually left them.

He went outside and sat on the step, quietly shutting the door. He needed to think, but his thinking time was interrupted when Señor Chapo came out to walk his dogs. Mario fell in stride. He took Ella's lead, so Hermanito could command all of Señor Chapo's attention. Carson probably saw them go by, but did not emerge. He and Ella were not on the best of terms; but Mario wasn't surprised when Pélon came out. While Ella was still in raptures over Pélon's arrival, Hermanito saw something of interest and hauled his owner across two lanes of traffic to investigate.

Mario took advantage of the privacy to ask Pélon, "Guess who I just found sacked out on the couch?"

"The guy who trashed your place? Hector maybe? I seen him sneak in apartments before."

"No, and he would not have needed my key. He's got one of his own."

"Right, then who was it?"

"Aunt Carmen. She's back. I don't think she trashed the place though.

I haven't talked to her yet. She's asleep."

Hermanito dragged Señor Chapo in shouting distance, so there wasn't time for more. Talk turned to baseball, Señor Chapo's second favorite thing.

When Mario got back home, his plan to clean was derailed because Aunt Carmen was up. She had changed into a flowered housecoat, and smelled of Prell.

"I was just about to call you in," she said. "How was school?"

"Fine," Mario said, wondering how to ask her about jail.

"Margarita had a little girl," Carmen said. "Fattest baby I ever saw. I told Margarita to go to the doctor and have her sugar checked, but she's got a hard head, that one, and doesn't trust American doctors. And this morning, after the baby made her appearance, I went to work. I was asleep on my feet when I came in, but not so tired I missed that you inhaled every scrap of food in the place. I'm glad we had a can of beans in the pantry. But why did you wash all the dishes? Did Hector fumigate?"

Mario took his plate to the stove, and heaped beans and Mexican rice and carnitas on it. Nothing had ever smelled as good.

"No fumigating," Mario said, as casually as he was able. "So, it was Margarita who had a baby. I wasn't sure you weren't arrested like that time Pélon's mother went after Pélon's Papi with that Louisville Slugger bat for drinking up the rent money."

Carmen laughed so hard her eyes watered, and she had to push back from the table to get control of herself. "Funny boy. You know perfectly well where I was. Not only did I tell Carson to tell you where I was, he watched that nice young policeman drop me off at her doorstep."

"What?" Mario said. "Oh, right." He did a pretty good job of keeping his head, which was suddenly rampant with thoughts of Carson's betrayal. It wasn't grown-up business, but something he would have to mull over with Pélon.

She changed the subject. "So you were a big shot and stayed here alone last night."

He hesitated, unsure which lie to tell. He sure couldn't tell her he slept in an alley. It would only be half a lie, because he was sure alone the night before. He didn't want to go into the mess the house had been in, tell the story of the disappeared key, or its mysterious return. In fact, he was itching for Carmen to go to bed, so he could go around the apartment and clean up the crumbs he'd dumped under the cushions, the mess swept under the rugs, and figure out what-all he'd tossed in the laundry hamper, because it had happened so fast, and there was a lot more in there than clothes.

After mass the next week, the priest called Mario aside. He was an old man who looked much like Mario imagined God might look, or a school principal. He was always a bit nervous when talking to the priest because it always seemed like he knew more about Mario than he was saying. And today felt like a bad day. He certainly didn't want to discuss old history like the men's magazine or his use of the word "fuck." Those were conversations he wished he could forget. But that's not the subject that came up.

"We have an opening for an altar boy," the priest said. He must have been impressed with Mario's crawl down the aisle, or else he'd mistaken the punishment for religious zeal. Or maybe, like Señor Chapo said, the priest had the hots for Aunt Carmen. Of course, Señor Chapo thought everybody had the hots for Aunt Carmen. Señor Chapo was a funny guy.

At first, Mario thought the priest's offer was the answer to his prayers. "How much does it pay?" he asked. It was a reasonable question. He had no idea why the priest looked so shocked.

"There is no pay," the priest said, taken aback.

He knew he had to watch his words. If he said too much, he'd embarrass his aunt. She was proud, and would never accept a handout. Worse, if the priest ever asked his aunt, she'd be thrilled at the honor. Plus, she was always trying to get on God's good side. She'd accept for him. But if Mario had to be at school and at church all of the time, when would he be able to earn money to keep them from losing the two bedroom?

"I don't think I will have the time," Mario said carefully and honestly. "I have to find a job to help out Aunt Carmen. But I don't want to get her hopes up, so its kind of a secret till I get paid." Which was all very true.

Coming home from church, he ran into Pélon, who was walking the neighborhood with his brothers. By themselves, they were a gang. Add in all their relatives, and they were a mob. Mostly, they made a big show to keep Vato's gang out of their block.

Sometimes Mario thought about joining a gang. It would be nice to belong to a group. Gangs had power. But his aunt was always telling him, "You can be friends with anyone you want, but you better not be part of any gang."

It was thanks to Pélon that Mario was able to get away with not joining a gang. Most of the Mexicans in the school expected you to be a part of a gang; it was an expectation, certainly, at ten and eleven and twelve to be part of one of the little kid gangs that merged with the other gangs as the kids got older. In East Los Angeles in 1959, there were a lot of neighborhood gangs. It was all about survival. They were all a lot of little gang-bangers like the ones in *West Side Story*, without all the singing and dancing.

Still, Mario got away with not joining a gang. The guys he went to school with, members of bigger gangs, didn't bother with him. They knew him, and they knew his big mouth. He didn't intimidate them either, not with his size; he was tall but all bones.

He was just plain and ordinary. It was Pélon who kept him out of trouble. Pélon was a trouble maker. It was a wonder they didn't expel him from school—probably lenience because he was so young. It wasn't just that Pélon could really put on a show. He could joke around, a joke for everything. But he was mean. Mario, who knew him better than anybody, couldn't even find words to express how mean Pélon was unless he started tossing out examples of horrible things he'd done. Mario wasn't at the top of the class but felt he was smarter than Pélon. He knew better than to tell that to his friend, or Pélon might smash a rock on his head, or kneecap him, as Mario had seen him do more than once. He wondered how someone who was as nice as Pélon's mom, who was like a second mom to Carson and him, could have raised such a psycho kid. Maybe he was like he was because of all the men his mom brought home. She was always falling for some broke, out-of-luck Prince Charming who would hang around until he popped her one.

All their Mexican friends came from poor families. As for Mario's Japanese friends, most of their parents owned businesses up and down First Street in Japantown. They lived in the better houses. Hardly any of them lived in apartments. Mario got along great with those guys. It was a different kind of relationship than with a person like Pélon who lived on his street.

As the days passed, his aunt never lost that look of worry. Mario was pressed to find a job, one way or another. Though he knew he shouldn't do it, he tried to talk his aunt into getting one of those color TVs from Dearden's. She told him no. A few days later, the Dearden's truck returned, and repossessed the black and white television. Mario didn't think she had done it to be mean, either because he heard her when she tried to talk the Dearden's driver into just waiting until Friday when she got paid, but he said his hands were tied. It wasn't his friend the roly-poly guy, either. It was the dumb one who didn't like ladders.

The house was extra quiet without the television. He was more convinced than ever that he had to bring some money home so his aunt would not worry anymore, and so they wouldn't have to lose any more of the furniture. His aunt's constant look of worry kept him up nights.

Mario had been thinking about Cosmo and his karate business. That was his best bet. The idea just came to him when he was watching Pélon bully the Japanese kids. He was watching not trying to stop him because when you said no to Pélon, he just got meaner. He felt guilty because he liked the Japanese kids, and he knew he was eventually going to have to go to church and confess. But that would be afterwards. Besides, it wasn't a racial thing. There was a purpose.

Pélon was a good friend, more like a brother than a friend. But he couldn't recall a time that he and Pélon had ever had a real argument. He might blow off some steam sometimes in Mario's direction, but never for real. He didn't want Pélon mad at him. Mario had seen Pélon cornered too many times. In a corner, Pélon was capable of anything. Mario had no intention of upsetting him and testing the limits of their brotherhood. Pélon had done some bad stuff, but Mario never told on him. He was lucky no one had ever asked, not even Aunt Carmen. He didn't think he could lie to Aunt Carmen.

At school, Mario saw Pélon provoking a Japanese friend. His name was Kenji. Mario went to Kenji and said, "Kenji how do you put up with this shit? Aren't you guys supposed to be all up with this self-defense thing? Aren't you supposed to know karate or judo or something? I know Pélon from way back, and if you stand up for yourself, he'll leave you alone."

"Who the heck knows," Kenji said. "My dad, he's got all sorts of belts, but he was raised in the old country. I'll kick this guy's ass if I have to. If it wasn't for that bunch that runs with him, I'd do it." He looked away, and looked back.

"If I knew how."

Mario was surprised that Kenji didn't know any self-defense. If his dad knew, why hadn't he taught him? The only kind of self defense any of them—even Pélon—knew, at least at that age, was to pick up a board and sling it at somebody and then run away. Or get a rock. Smash it against a guy's head, which Pélon had done more than once, just because he was mean, and wanted to. Kenji wasn't a rock-smasher, but he was ripe to be sold on lessons. Mario thought it was true, that Kenji probably could take down Pélon—if Pélon was ever alone, and if he ever was going to fight fair. But like Kenji said, Pélon, he always had his little gang with him.

"I know a guy gives lessons in fighting."

"What kind of fighting?"

"Your kind," Mario said. "It's not like boxing. It's that Japanese fighting. The guy's named Cosmo over on Brooklyn. I could probably get you a deal on classes."

"If I wanted to do that, I'd ask my dad."

"And say what? That you're scared a little guy like Pélon is gonna take you down?"

Kenji didn't really want to tell his dad he was being bullied at school but he didn't want to ask for lessons either.

"My dad always talks about the dojo back when he was a kid." Kenji told him. "I figure if he wanted me to know karate, he'd teach me himself."

Mario had seen Kenji's father. He might be Cosmo's age, but he was a round and soft businessman, not a teacher of martial arts.

It just happened that over the course of a few more days, Pélon picked on Kenji a couple more times, the way he picked on all the guys who weren't on their street. Once he took Kenji's ice cream sandwich at lunch, in front of a whole table full of Japanese kids. And that ice cream had not only cost him five cents, he had to clean his plate of a particularly nasty liver lunch. He had to put a whole piece of liver and a bunch of green beans in his milk carton and not get caught by the lunch lady.

When Kenji finally came back to Mario and told him he'd sign up, three other Japanese kids with him said they'd do it too. They'd all been sitting at the same lunch table. They'd all lost their ice cream, lunch money, their homework, or their pride to Pélon at one time or another.

Mario went back to Cosmo, and said to Cosmo, "So how much would you charge for lessons?"

"Two dollars a lesson."

"I see. And what do I get if I bring you some customers?"

"If you bring me enough customers, you get a job."

"What could I be doing here anyway? I mean, cleaning up this little place? Take me ten minutes."

So Cosmo said, "Tell you what, Mario. For every dollar I make, I'm going to give you ten percent."

Math was never Mario's subject.

"Ten percent, what is that?"

Cosmo offered, "Well, I'll give you ten cents."

"Ten cents? I can't buy shit with ten cents."

Cosmo made a choking sound and put his hand over his mouth. If Mario hadn't known better, he'd have thought Cosmo was laughing. When Cosmo put his hand down, he had a perfect poker face. So Mario knew he'd been mistaken. Even a little kid like Mario knew that a professional like Cosmo wouldn't laugh while doing a business deal.

Mario continued, seriously, "You give me fifty cents for every two dollars you make off of me. For as long as I get you customers."

Cosmo whistled. "And if you bring me nobody, you get nothing. It's a deal."

Mario figured that Cosmo figured Mario was crazy. How did he think Mario was going to get these customers? But right away, Mario brought in Kenji and his 3 friends. And before the week was out, Mario brought in a dozen more, all of them Japanese. Was Cosmo happy? He was over the moon. Was Mario the hero? Absolutely.

Mario did some fast talking with every new student and got other family members. Brothers, sisters, friends. Even parents sometimes, homesick for the old ways. He even got a bunch of fifteen—it was a whole family, down to the brothers, sons, father, uncles and even a grandfather. (Though when Mario watched, all the gramps did during the class was sip tea and bow a lot.)

Then those friends each brought one or two more to join, all of them giving Mario credit. Mario lost track of his percent for each dollar that he made because, well, math. All he knew was that he was paid in folding money, not change.

When Cosmo paid him, the first thing Mario did was go down to Dearden's. He stopped to look at the color TV but now that he was a working man, he could see his aunt was right about it being expensive. He paid the back payment on the TV and made the rest of their payment, too, as long as he was there. He talked to the roly-poly guy, his friend, who made sure the driver promised to deliver it that day. He went back to the apartment and waited around, wanting to see his aunt's face when they brought back the TV. He didn't tell her what he had done, but all through dinner he was too excited to eat her delicious frijoles. Finally after dark, the Dearden's truck arrived, and they brought the TV in. His aunt was speechless. On the way out, the driver said "Goodbye, Mr. Luna." Then it all hit the fan.

"How did that man know you, Mario?" It was never a good thing when Aunt Carmen used that tone of voice.

"I saw him before," Mario said evasively. He hadn't thought about this. He thought she'd be so happy to get the TV back that she'd skip giving him the third degree.

"Before, when?" Aunt Carmen was like a bulldog when she had her mind set. And she had her mind set on getting to the bottom of this.

"Before. When I was at Dearden's."

He didn't meet her eyes. He started staring at his tennis shoes and noticed one of them was untied. He bent down and tied his shoe. When he looked up, Aunt Carmen was still glaring at him. She speared him with a look.

"And what were you doing there?"

"Paying the bill," he capitulated.

"And where did you get the money?"

"I've been working for Cosmo after school. Cosmo, the karate teacher. I was going to tell you. It's a surprise."

"You are ten years old! How can you have a job?"

She must have had a million reasons why he couldn't work. For each one he gave, she threw back three. Then finally, he was down to his one real reason—they needed the money. They argued over the job until she sent him to bed early. He turned off the lights, crawled under his sheets and lay there listening to the silent apartment. Then he saw a bit of flickering light from under his door, and if he listened very closely, he could hear the sound of the television. Very quietly, he opened the door and peeked out, seeing his aunt seated in the comfortable chair, her face bathed in the flickering black and white light. Mario couldn't see the screen from where he was, but he could see his aunt's face, and she looked more relaxed than he'd seen her all week.

He fell asleep with a smile on his face. He knew he had done the right thing.

The next morning, he was not so sure. The conflict over his job went on for days. During and after school, Mario kept working at getting students for Cosmo. The rest of the time, he and Carmen were like two stone walls, neither budging an inch because of the stubbornness they shared. If either of them wrapped their mind around something, they were on it like a dog with a bone. Neither knew the meaning of giving up. There was argument; there was silence. There was argument again. There was an uneasy week.

They were at an impasse until Señor Chapo decided to step in. On the face of it, his arrival was not unusual. Lots of the time, he came over for dinner. Typically, he would buy an enormous beef roast or a turkey or a ham, and would knock on the door to say it was way too much for one person, so would Aunt Carmen cook it? Always with a bottle of wine as well. Then Aunt Carmen would return the favor, and cook way too much of something so she could invite him over in return. It was a charade that happened several times in a normal week. This week was not normal. Like his dogs, Señor Chapo heard everything through the wall and didn't pretend he didn't. He did not come over until after there were a few days of deafening silence.

Mario opened the door to the familiar knock.

"Mario, do you think your Aunt Carmen knows how to fix Cornish game hens?"

Mario backed away from the door and retreated into his room. Aunt Carmen could speak for herself.

Señor Chapo had chosen well; the hens were several but small, and took maybe an hour to turn golden brown and succulent. He left and returned with a bottle of sangria. It was a relief to have the Señor at the table, chatting as if everything were hunky dory.

Señor Chapo poured wine for Carmen and soda for Mario. He portioned out the hens, giving two to Mario, who had never had them before. He provided at least some conversation, as he talked alternately to Carmen and Mario. Some people sulked when they were angry. Some people cleaned. Some people ironed. Aunt Carmen cooked. The ambiance was uncomfortable, but the meal was splendid. Mario had the standing option to either cook or clean; so afterwards, sullenly, Mario was stuck washing dishes after dinner. He wiped the last fork, and put it away.

"What's My Line" was on. Bennet Cerf had said something funny, and the studio audience roared with laughter. Not so the adults on the sofa. They were speaking seriously, and so softly that Mario had to turn the water off to hear what they were saying. No surprise that the topic of conversation was his job.

"He's too young to work," Carmen said. "Children don't have any business working. It is my responsibility to provide for him. Sometimes it just kills me. I had it all."

"You still have it all."

Carmen responded to something so quietly, Mario had to employ his secret weapon directly, and stand under the vent. He grabbed a glass and started wiping it with a towel in case his aunt decided to look in. But she hadn't moved, and she was still talking. He kept wiping and listening.

"No, I really did have it all. I had a bag of money I lugged around for years."

"A bag of money," Señor Chapo said. "Really."

"It was maybe a million dollars. I carried it around for four years, in fact. The money was for Mario. For his future. But there were these drug punks after us, and I just couldn't take it any more. Don't look at me like that. What, you don't believe me?"

"I believe you," Señor Chapo said, but his voice was skeptical. Mario felt skeptical too, and thought maybe Aunt Carmen had swallowed too much of that red wine she liked.

"If I hadn't thrown it in his face, we could be living in the best house in town, instead of struggling week to week, wondering where the next month is coming from. But no. I had to be a big shot and give it back. If I could go back in time, I'd kick my own ass."

Mario's jaw dropped. So did the glass he was wiping.

"What's going on in there?"

Mario grabbed a broom and dustpan, and, well away from the vent, answered. "Sorry, dropped a glass."

"Be careful!"

Mario swept up the glass, still listening. Carmen went back to talking about the money. She did sound drunk.

Señor Chapo let her go on like this for a while, and said only one thing.

"I don't know about the money, but about the boy and his job, let him be a man."

So eventually, even though Aunt Carmen didn't like surprises and she knew he was way too young to be working, thanks to Señor Chapo, she relented.

Mario said nothing of the conflict at home. The next time he saw Cosmo, he said, "Let me just continue to get business for you. I know a lot of kids. I'm probably screwing myself, but give me ten dollars a week."

Mario figured if he could get ten dollars a week, that would be helpful at home, and take care of him, and maybe he could save up for a car.

So Cosmo said, "Promotion. Getting me business is called promotion."

He didn't think about it for long. Besides, what was there to think about? How could he lose?

"Ok."

"As long as this continues, as long as you promote for me, as long as I have the income, I'll give you ten dollars a week. But you gotta show up. And here is the condition." Cosmo said, "Ya gotta go in and take a class. Every day."

Mario said, "Why?"

He said, "That's the condition. You want ten dollars a week? That's what you got."

Mario figured his Auntie made about forty dollars a week now. She used to bring home fifty in cash until the company had been forced to cut back on overtime and put her on payroll. Now that they took out taxes, it was harder to get by. Mario figured he could make ten dollars. Not as much as his aunt but it was enough to make up the difference of what they had lost, and then some. He didn't have to go downtown. He didn't have to take a bus. All he had to do is come up to Brooklyn Avenue, take a few classes and continue to get Cosmo some business.

"Okay Cosmo, I don't know why you want me to, but I'll do that. I can get you more students. I have an idea about signs."

Cosmo laughed. He said, "Where do you get these ideas? Get the signs, I'll pay for them."

The idea hadn't been far fetched. Mario went to school with a boy named Richard, whose father owned a printing press company on First Street. Richard was short, and chubby, and wore thick glasses. He came to school every day with ink-stained fingers. He was a little kid who did a man's job, and knew it. He took school very seriously, because his work relied on his being able to spell well, and do math, and think like a grown-up. Richard was one of the kids who was not in a gang, but he would print cards and signs for anybody who would pay for it. Ever since Mario could remember, Richard worked at his dad's shop setting the printing press stuff for invitations and other things for the community. It's not like there were a lot of neighborhood print shops.

Mario told Richard what was needed. And while he was talking, you know Mario, he was just talking, man to man, doing business with Richard. Richard was talking, man to man, doing business with Mario.

Richard mentioned the difficulties of getting ink off his hands, though he sounded a little boastful when he said it. He let Mario behind the counter to take a look at the print press. Mario was suitably impressed, and came up with some working man type complaints too.

"I have to find new batches of people to take classes," Mario said. "Not just all the Japanese kids in our grade, but older kids. And younger ones."

Mario said, "It's difficult explaining sometimes. I have to show them they need the class. I have to bring them up to the shop."

Richard was also a businessman. He knew when he smelled business.

"I'll make you some signs. Print you some flyers that say Self-defense, karate. And put the address on Brooklyn. You can put them up, you know, where ever. And, take a look at these." Richard handed Mario a stack of little white cards that said "Brooklyn Print Shop" and beneath it had Richard's name. "I can make up some of these for you."

Mario said, "Yeah. Yeah, I need those little cards. I want you to put on there, Mario Luna. Put something about self-defense, karate or something."

"Yeah, I got just the thing," Richard said, thumbing through a big book that had different writing styles like Bodini Bold, Block, Futura, and Gothic. He turned to a page with stick figures, and pointed one out to Mario. "I'll tell you what. I can even put on this picture of a guy doing karate."

Mario wasn't sure if the figure was doing karate or ballet, but said, "Yeah, do that."

So Mario got his signs. He distributed them. He put them up in the barber shops. A couple of store owners in Japanese town let him put signs up even though the signs were in English.

When he saw them, Cosmo loved the cards.

"I'll pay for the cards too, or whatever you're going to do. That's called advertising."

"Oh," Mario said. "Ok. Advertising."

He might not be so great in the classroom, but this was the kind of educational moment that really stuck with Mario.

Everything wasn't perfect; Mario made a mistake because the signs and cards didn't have Cosmo's phone number. On the cards, it wasn't a mistake because Mario and his aunt didn't even have a telephone. Mario started passing cards around. He started promoting Cosmo, almost to everybody.

He ran out of boys his age. Pretty soon, he asked the girls if they'd do it. Not many of the girls that he knew of took lessons. Cosmo would teach a girl if she wanted to study, just like he would have in their country. Some girls were interested, though. Like the boys, the girls brought their sisters, their friends, their aunts, their mothers.

Not a single Mexican or black kid could afford the lessons. Tortuga only took occasional lessons that Mario occasionally offered him. (Mario felt that Tortuga and his two left feet needed all the help he could get.)

Each time he got paid, Mario realized how lucky he was that there were so many Japanese kids in school. He'd even heard from friends of some of the fathers he had signed up to brush up or to learn. Many were proud that their kids were taking the classes like they had back in Japan.

So by the end of the fourth or fifth month, maybe six months after this, Cosmo was smoking. He was busy. Cosmo gave Mario a little raise. An extra dollar. At the end of a year, he gave him a second raise, and started paying Mario twenty dollars a week.

One Saturday when he was taking his regular lesson, Mario was shocked when his Aunt Carmen actually came to the studio and watched his lesson. Afterwards, she sat down with Cosmo wearing a determined look on her face that Mario well knew. The truth was that, Señor Chapo notwithstanding, Aunt Carmen had never reconciled herself to Mario having a job at ten—now eleven—years old. Cosmo went on and on to his aunt about Mario's talent, how he was a salesman, a natural. Mario didn't hear any more, because Aunt Carmen sent him outside so he couldn't hear anything. He knew he shouldn't have been surprised—Aunt Carmen had always looked out for him. Knowing how she was, what could she do but go to the studio and check Cosmo out for herself? He was surprised she had taken so long to do it.

He waited outside patiently. At least, he would have looked patient to anyone watching. A year's worth of classes had taught him something. He was anxious, and burned that anxiety by doing a move while standing on the sidewalk, looking in. He could see his reflection almost like the mirror in the studio, but he could make out Aunt Carmen deep in conversation with Cosmo. He could also see in the plate glass that Tortuga had joined him and was practicing a move. Kenji, whose class had just finished, also joined in, with a couple of others who gathered in the alley and a parking lot. People outside were pulling over to watch. Mario scarcely noticed, as his attention was on Aunt Carmen, who was finally finished with her talk. Mario broke off his workout. Kenji started to show off. Tortuga couldn't keep up, fell over, and watched from the ground.

Aunt Carmen reached the door and opened it, startled by the crowd of rubberneckers. Her color was high. She stopped abruptly, and looked at the crowd, now standing around Kenji, who was doing a complicated kata, or series of moves. Kenji improvised a big finale that he made up out of his own head, and everyone, including Mario, clapped.

"I'll see you at home," Carmen said, and left.

Mario went in to touch base with Cosmo.

"So that's your aunt. At least she is real. She's not at all what I pictured."

Aunt Carmen was about twice as tall as Cosmo, and not half his age.

Over dinner, Carmen admitted to Mario that she had followed him that first week and looked over the shop. It was close by, and it seemed safe enough; and the work Mario was doing, whatever it was, did not seem to be interfering with his schoolwork. She just couldn't figure out what that work was.

She admitted, after she finally met Cosmo, that the little Japanese businessman had taken her by surprise. He wasn't what she had pictured, either. He had shown her the figures of Mario's percentage which Carmen understood with no problem—she was an accountant, after all. All the math brains Mario didn't have, Carmen had in spades.

"Why did he think you—we—used to be homeless?" Carmen asked.

"I don't know," Mario said. "I'll be sure to find out."

She admitted that the idea that an eleven year old was making twenty dollars a week for a couple of hours of work when she herself only made fifty for forty hours was still hard for her to take. She saw him carrying the business cards and putting up posters. She didn't see him doing anything illegal. No drugs, no robbery, and he still went to church. He brought the money home. She made an agreement that Mario would keep a couple of bucks for pocket change, which would help her because she didn't have to give Mario anything. When she was short on bills, she would use his money to make up the difference; and the rest of it she would save so that when Mario got old enough to buy a car, he could.

So Mario said, "Fine." But he suggested, "Look, take a couple of dollars a week more toward our Deardon's payment, and that way we can keep buying furniture."

His aunt laughed.

"Mario, our apartment's so small, where would we put it?" Her talk with Cosmo had tempered her a bit. She still shook her head in disbelief over this little boy successfully getting business for a grown businessman.

"I don't know, maybe we can move to a bigger place." Mario was thinking about that bigger, more expensive apartment the landlord had said was going to be available. "Maybe Cosmo would find a way to pay me more money if I keep getting more business." But that's just the way Mario thought.

Chapter 3
1964
Mario

Even though Mario never really took karate to heart, by the time he was fourteen, he was pretty good, good enough to earn some belts and recognition along the way, but there were always more to work toward. He really never tried for the belts, but he did kick butt when he was on the mat.

Most of the Japanese guys in his school were regulars now at Cosmo's and could do the same things he could. It was part of the routine, and there was a trick to it anyway, all concentration and discipline. Sometimes Mario was surprised he could do what he could, since he didn't know how much he really concentrated, how much discipline he really had. What he did have was a lot of practice.

The closest he came to showing off is when his aunt attended a couple of tournaments, somewhere away from East Los Angeles. Las Vegas. Northern California. Cosmo sponsored all of his students. Some parents drove their cars. Mario rode with somebody. His aunt rode with somebody.

His aunt was there. She, who had never missed a work day as long as he knew her took off work to be at his tournaments, it was that important to her. She was so proud when he was on the mat that she was beaming. He was so much bigger than the other boys his age, he felt like he had an advantage and others had a disadvantage. It was almost like Hermanito going after Ella. But that was not always true. A little guy from another city was far advanced, and did some number on him, almost knocked him out with a flip he had not anticipated. He didn't hold a grudge. It wasn't just that he figured to learn from his mistakes. It's that karate was never his objective. It was never about the "sport," and always about the business of the job.

Still, he did learn some important lessons: first, that he was not ever going to let down his guard; second, that he was not ever going in thinking he was going to win at the sport. He went in playing a different game entirely. Being in the tournament would help him get more business for Cosmo. Everything was going to be a challenge, but while everyone else's goal at the tourney was to win, his goal was to get business. He had no opposition. That became the way he approached situations: the angle that meant there was no competition.

Time passed, and he grew more. At six foot two in his bare feet, his friends constantly kidded him about his size. After taking up karate, the ribbing was not just about his height. None of them had really stripped until they got to junior high school and had gym class. Even if they were not fags, they looked at each other. They were careful not to get caught looking. Let's just say that in the showers, Mario's size was legendary. Karate gave him an athlete's physique. But nature gave him the particular endowment which would be an asset in Mario's adult life.

By fourteen, Mario had a favorite girl, though he wasn't really going out. He knew not just the girls in his class, but the names of the ones who hid in Hollenbeck Park when they were on break. And they knew him, not as a paying customer, but the cute kid they'd like to go out with, if they did things like going out on real dates for fun. The corner girls had names like Hershey, Cotton Candy, Candy Cane, Strawberry Bite, Cherry, Cinnamon, Honey, Lolly, Lemondrop, and Pixie. When he wasn't in school, running errands for Aunt Carmen, or hustling for Cosmo, he liked to hang out with the corner girls, especially Pixie.

Cosmo had given Mario a bonus because he'd made a good business move at a tournament. He took a fall, just so he could talk a kid who wasn't from their neighborhood into taking Cosmo's class. The kid had been a gateway to a whole new different school of kids, and dozens of new students, so far.

Mario might be becoming a peerless businessman, but he'd taken his extra dollars and bought boxes of a bunch of different candies from Safeway. He was still a kid. Because it was right after Halloween, everything was on sale. It was almost more than he could carry, and he could carry a lot.

It was a long walk back from Brooklyn, and as he was taking a shortcut, Mario passed Officer Dibble asleep in his squad car. At first, he seemed to be asleep. His eyes were closed and he was leaning back, but his hands were gripping the steering wheel. Then Mario saw he wasn't alone. Someone's head popped up. One of the corner girls was in the passenger seat of the squad car. Mario walked up, and Dibble and the girl both waved.

"Want some candy?" Mario said, not that he really wanted to offer it, but it seemed polite. He hoped Honey wasn't getting arrested again. Dibble was always getting pushed to arrest the corner girls. When there was some big sting coming down, Dibble and a few of the other beat cops tried to keep the corner girls out of it.

"No thanks," Dibble said. "I don't think I should be eating candy during an arrest."

"I should say not," Honey said kindly. "You have your professional decorum to consider. So, did you try what I suggested?"

"It worked like a charm," Dibble said. "She had a smile on her face."

"Officer Dibble is a newlywed," Honey explained.

"Congratulations," Mario said.

"Sometimes he comes to me for advice in the new wife department," Honey said.

"You don't say," Mario said. "So you know about new wives?"

"Sweetie, I know it all," Honey said. "I know how to make 'em happy. I know how to keep 'em happy."

"I believe her," Dibble said. He was looking flushed and sweaty for November, and some of his buttons were undone. It was obvious Dibble had been having a little refreshment.

"I'll take a Bit-O-Honey, if you have one," Honey said. Her lipstick was smeared.

Mario wiped his mouth. Honey got the message and looked at herself in her compact.

"Oh my," she said, "I wonder how that happened." She flashed Mario a big smile, and fixed her makeup. Mario had never seen anyone chewing on candy at the same time they applied lipstick.

"I do love a Bit-O-Honey," she said.

"Just like your name," Mario said.

"It's a shame you weren't selling candy," Officer Dibble said, a little breathlessly, like he'd been running. "Selling candy isn't illegal."

"What's to say I wasn't?" Honey said. "I sure was selling a Bit-O-Honey. And making a personal delivery, too. My civic duty." This time she smiled at Dibble who flushed beet red with embarrassment.

"I do hate to interfere with free enterprise," Officer Dibble said.

"Mario, Big Man, I see you have a whole box of Bit-O-Honey. I'll give you twice the price on the side of the box," Honey said. "And I bet I know some girls who'd do the same, if you explain it to them. I think we're all going to be selling candy from here on out."

Being a businessman, Mario agreed it was a brilliant idea.

"Here let me buy that for you," Dibble said, handing Honey a wad of cash. Half of it disappeared down Honey's cleavage before she handed to Mario.

Mario couldn't turn it down. He liked the idea of helping the girls. Plus, she was offering twice what he'd paid, and he still had another box of Bit-O-Honey. Plus he shouldn't turn down Dibble. He paid the girls a visit, made a quick explanation about their new sideline, sold them all the candy he had, and walked back to Brooklyn to buy out the rest of the Halloween stock. After that, the corner girls would sometimes borrow money from him or get him to deliver the sweets to supply their candy business cover. All this because Mario happened to be walking by when Officer Dibble had told them to clean up their act. Not one of them had gotten arrested after they started selling candy at 4th and Soho, even during the day.

Businesswise, Mario was doing well. He kept bringing in new clients. When he ran out of friends to send, he got them from other places. He used his gift of gab to convince owners and managers to let him put up signs, and peppered neighborhoods near and far, windows, mailboxes, bulletin boards and under the windshield wipers of the cars parked in countless parking lots. When the school year started, there were always a couple of new kids, their friends, their brothers—even their sisters—to convince that karate was the way to go.

Cosmo was on him all the time to keep up all his responsibilities. If Mario wanted to get paid, not only did he have to come to class, he had to work out. Cosmo didn't believe in weights for his formal classes, but Mario was his poster boy, and special to him. He was still too skinny, not so much because they didn't have that much money to do too much eating, but mostly because he was growing. Mario didn't know what Cosmo was trying to make of him, but sometimes he felt like a human bonsai.

Mario, Pélon, Tortuga, Carson and an assortment of the guys sometimes frequented a basketball court down at the Jewish community center on Soto. But mainly Mario worked out at Cosmo's with sit ups and weights. Sit ups were easy. Mario would just fantasize about girls. About all kinds of things. He could do sit up after sit up. Two hundred, three hundred. His stomach became tight like a washboard. Cosmo didn't want him to become too muscular for karate so he coached him, gave just enough weights to tone him, but at fourteen, he was buff. Mario didn't want to look too good because looking too good would only anger his friends. Still, Mario had to admit he was a little excited, a little proud of himself, but not cocky. You couldn't get too cocky when Pélon was your friend. Pélon could cut you down to size in a heartbeat.

His aunt and he did ok, especially with the extra money. She still was delivering the occasional baby, not that she ever got paid for it. At least he was old enough to stay alone, and not to assume that if she didn't come home, she'd been arrested.

He put away lots of food without it ever showing up, except that he was always getting taller, and his twin bed seemed to be shrinking. He had to take off the footboard so he could stretch out. They were still in that same two bedroom apartment. Aunt Carmen smiled more than she used to. She was proud of him, but she was always worried about money. How could Cosmo keep paying so much? Twenty dollars a week now. It was a fortune. She saved it.

In ninth grade, the year he was fourteen, his first period class was English. His eyes nearly popped out of his head the first time he saw his fresh-out-of-college teacher, Mrs. Maloney. He didn't sit in the back of the class where all the black kids were in their jeans and t-shirts, or in the middle with all of the Hispanic kids who were, like him, wearing chinos and t-shirts. He sat up front with all the Japanese kids in their jeans and plaid button-downs. Mrs. Maloney was strict as hell, and he still hated English class, but she was some serious eye candy. Some mornings he saw her husband dropping her off at the school. He was a *gabacho*.

Some of the people at school called Mario a con. They didn't say it hatefully. He understood what a con was. You couldn't live in his neighborhood and not know what a con was—but he wasn't a con. He wasn't out to cheat or swindle anybody. He was just good with his mouth. He could sell. Mario realized he could sell anything. He tried a couple of times to interest the slow markets down Brooklyn Avenue to do the same kind of promotion for them as he did for Cosmo. They were too cheap to make it worth his while; they had no vision. They didn't understand what he was able to do. Mario gave up on them. He hadn't tried that any more, now that he was making twenty-five or thirty dollars plus some bonuses from Cosmo. If Mario was busted, Cosmo would give him an extra two or three dollars. He always made sure Mario had money in his pocket. He knew the situation at home. He knew that Mario gave all of his pay to his aunt, except for a couple of bucks he held out for cigarettes, beer and stuff.

Mario thought that if he hadn't had Cosmo, he might have been like Pélon and his brothers, always cruising for trouble. Cosmo kept him too busy to get into mischief. More importantly, Cosmo gave him some kind of a yard stick to measure himself. Pélon didn't have a yardstick. He was always proving himself, every day, always fighting to prove he was man enough. When you're king of the mountain like that, king of the neighborhood, you always have to fight to stay top dog. But Mario—he didn't have to prove himself. With the karate, and the working out, with Cosmo's confidence in him, and especially with the way his auntie now treated him like a man full grown, Mario didn't need to fight everybody all the time.

He knew who he was. He also knew he had a knack that helped him get by. He could persuade people, even Pélon, when he set his mind to it. Besides, it's not like he was hurting for money. There was enough money for food, and decent clothes. Nothing too fine, though. Nothing that would get Vago's attention.

Vago was a guy from a few blocks over, a guy from an older kid gang, a real *desgraciado*. These bad boys came and went, fighters who live in the moment, and get to be top dog until the next *desgraciado* topples him off the hill. He ran with his own gang, and had a reputation for just taking things. Word was he was known for being the kind of guy who would take candy from babies just because he could, the same way Pélon was known for his hair-trigger temper and quick defense of his friends and turf. Vago was the reason the corner girls were so tight with Pelon's big brothers. They gave the girls free protection on account of their being such good friends. Once in a while Vago drifted too far West from his neighborhood right into Pélon's turf and bothered someone in the vicinity of Chicago and 4th; and when that happened, Pélon took it on himself to see it didn't happen again.

All Mario knew was that Pélon had missed a day of school. The next thing, Carson told him that the gangs were going to have it out at Hollenbeck Park. Carson had become part of Pélon's gang, but he had changed from his former talkative self to one who kept a low profile. He didn't talk a lot of shit. When he opened his mouth, he had something to say. He didn't get into anyone's face like Pélon and most of the others. He just hung around probably because it was safer than not. Mario saw more of Carson in Junior High than before. Carson was clean cut, and wore well ironed khakis and shined shoes though he claimed he only had two pair of pants. Carson always carried a comb so that when he sat, he had the habit of running the comb down the pleat to keep it pressed. Everyone made fun of him for doing this; he'd respond with a smile or give the finger. No one dared to take offense because he was on Pélon's inner circle.

It was Carson who told Mario that something was going to happen. Mario never heard exactly what started it.

This was one of those times that Mario decided Pélon needed persuading. As soon as he heard it was going down, Mario got in gear to stop the conflict. First he went off to find Pixie.

Pixie was at the house off Chicago where the corner girls stayed, a big rabbit warren of a lumpy, ramshackle wood frame house with rooms haphazardly added on by random carpenters over the years. It was painted the colors of ice cream, and owned by a not-quite retired ladybird everyone called Nana. She was old as time, did exactly as she wanted, and never said no to the girls she took under her wing. There was nothing wrong with her heart, but her house would have been better off if she'd hired better carpenters. Nana saw to it that none of her girls had anyone to answer to, and that there was always food to eat, and a warm bed to sleep in. She maintained a rainy day fund of bail-out money. Officer Dibble had even been known to bring her a lost soul instead of hauling her in for doing her job. It was morning, and the place seemed deserted. The big wooden door was unlocked, and Mario made his way through the cavernous entry down a snaky hall to a downstairs level where he found Pixie in her room, still asleep in her birthday suit after a late night. He woke her up with a honeybun, and she returned the favor; before he left, he told her to warn the corner girls to steer clear of the park.

He tried slipping out without getting noticed, but Nana had an uncanny sense, or maybe it was the old lapdog she carried around with her. It was a tiny mutt named Dolly, like Elle Grande, teacup-sized, but unlike her, silent. Like Nana's girls, Dolly had once been a stray, with most of the life beaten out of her, but now they were both ancient and inseparable. Nana could turn no one away, not even an unwanted dog more dead than alive. She was friends with a neighbor woman who had a house full of cats, and another who never turned away a dog. Nana just opened her house and heart to two-legged strays.

Dolly watched the world from bulging coffee-brown Ping-Pong ball eyes, and communicated with Nana almost mystically. Mario's hand was almost on the door knob, but like a wraith, a silk flowered robe wafted out of the kitchen into the hall. Nana, in the robe, called his name.

"Coffee, Mario?" Nana emerged from the kitchen with a cup, and holding an aluminum coffee pot, the kind that perked on the stove, and smelled better than any coffee ever tasted.

Like the house, Nana's hair was always the color of some kind of ice cream. Sometimes it was white. Today it was orange sherbet, in tight pin curls with some kind of loose, brightly patterned scarf draped over all.

"No time, Nana," Mario inhaled appreciatively, and said, "I already told Pixie this, but if you get a chance, tell the girls to avoid the park today. I hear something might be going down."

Nana fluttered nervously. "Thanks for the heads up."

She stepped into the kitchen and set the coffee on the gas burner; and while her back was turned, Mario slipped some bills into the cookie jar. She saw him do it, reflected in the toaster.

Before she turned around, he was already outside on the front walk. He thought he heard her say, "Such a good boy."

Then he went to Pélon's, hoping to catch him at home; thirty seconds later, and he would have missed him. He was going into Pélon's just about the same time Pélon was heading out. Mario pretended to block the door. Pélon just backed up and sat down in the mirror image of Mario's living room (except Pélon's was smoky and crowded and none too clean since his overworked mother was working two jobs to feed her household of hungry sons, and had no time for such things as sweeping and taking out garbage.) The current boyfriend was hacking up lugies in the bathroom.

Pélon did not want to listen to reason.

"Hey man, why would you want to go to juvenile hall? Why would you want to piss it all away, being in jail, what are you going to prove? And what about your mom? I mean, come on. Somebody could really get hurt. Let's be done with these wars."

Pélon didn't exactly agree with Mario's logic, but he didn't go to the park either. Mario went over to Cosmo's for a bit, and then walked home. He didn't mind the walk, although the sidewalks were in dire need of repair. A person could trip just walking down the crumbling sidewalk. He really needed to be careful where he put his feet.

The wooden houses and plastered apartment buildings on both sides of Chicago Street were older homes from the thirties, all of them with a little yard in front, some with nice grass, others with dying grass or none at all. Unlike Nana's place, most of the buildings had needed a paint job for years, but the only significance of that to Mario was that he might be able to get paid for painting—if they paid enough—though he was more likely to give such a job to one of Pélon's friends. Some of the more prosperous homeowners had added siding over the old wood frames. Others had plastered over the frame. Some appeared to be new structures, but the new was only skin deep. He was nearly home when who should come his way but Vago.

Mario tried the same approach with Vago as he had with Pélon, but Vago only laughed at him. With four buddies to back him, Vago was awfully brave.

"Whatcha think you are, a counselor? I should kick your ass, man. If we want to brawl, we're going to, and you can't stop us."

Vago would never have come into this neighborhood without his gangbangers. Mario wasn't about to be intimidated. He was easily twice the size of any of these guys, and what's more, he knew how to defend himself.

"We don't want a fight here."

"Yeah, man, I'll kick your ass, and then I'll start on Pélon."

Vago stepped up like he was going to crowd Mario, but Mario wasn't the type to get crowded. He set his feet. Mario looked down at him in a way that he knew would piss Vago off and poked his chest really hard with one finger. It wasn't a lot of effort but it was exactly in the sternum. Sometimes this sweating for Cosmo really paid off. It made him back off.

Vago said "Urp," went two shades of gray, and tried to look invincible while struggling for air.

"Back off, jerkwad," Mario said. "I'm tired of hearing your shit. Tired of hearing how you pick on people. Tired of hearing it, tired of seeing your face and the faces of your four musketeers."

Vago scowled at him. It was a mean look.

"Sissy," he said to Mario. "If you didn't have Pélon at your back, you'd be walking around with a cane, if you were walking at all."

Mario looked to the left. He looked to the right. He made a big show of looking behind him.

"Pélon? I don't see Pélon."

It was an invitation Vago couldn't resist. Like one of Cosmo's beginners, his eyes telegraphed his target. Vago charged like an angry bull. This time Mario didn't even have to lift a finger. He stepped out of the way. Vago overshot his mark and fell on his face. He was sure it had been an accident, so he clambered up and charged Mario again, this time missing Mario and slamming into the corner fence post. He wasn't quite so fast to get up. He staggered, and shook his head. His tough bunch of four gangbangers suddenly looked a lot like fifteen year old boys. Mario heard them whispering something amongst themselves about Brooklyn Avenue and Cosmo's karate school. He noticed they all kept their distance, too. He didn't think he should crack a smile and spoil the moment. Businessman that he was, he thought seriously about giving them one of his karate cards. Not that they could pay for lessons. If they hadn't been with Vago, he would have. Unwilling to leave a trail to exactly where he lived, he stood his ground while they walked off. After they rounded the corner, he could hear Vago bitching out his companions for not backing him up.

Mario considered that he'd been awfully lucky to come through without a scratch. By now the gangs carried their own little arsenals—hammers, car jacks, baseball bats, heavy chains, and whatever else might be handy and lethal. Other gangs—older kids—in the same neighborhood carried guns as protection against gangs from other neighborhoods who even had rifles. It was scary. It was like living in a jungle where the animals carried weapons and didn't stay in cages.

Mario didn't know if Pélon and Vago admired or resented him, but at least everybody was alive to have an afterwards. The wars wouldn't be over but that particular one was. Except for that time, he stayed away from the gangs. He did not stay away from Pélon. Pélon was his friend—like his bodyguard. Half his size, but he was his bodyguard. Imagine that. It's hard to explain how such a little guy was so significant, but that was just Pélon. It was just he ran around with so much power. Pélon had been arrested probably twenty times, and they kept sending him right home to his mother.

Pelon's mom's latest boy friend, the one with a big smoking addiction, was called Sandor. He was big as a phone booth, dumb as a brick, and built like a traffic cone. When Mario got home, Sandor was hanging out on the stoop of the apartment, picking at Pélon about not going to stand up for himself over the gang conflict at Hollenbeck Park. Mario didn't know how the old guy was clever enough to know about the fight that didn't happen, and stupid enough to pick at Pélon.

Mario walked up in time to see it happening, but was too far off to help.

Pelon's mom came out, still a little bit of a woman with hair so big it was a miracle she could hold up her head, and a blast of a voice, like the

Queen Mary, moored in Long Beach.

"Leave my boy alone!" she roared, a vibrating blast that shivered the windows for two blocks. She wedged her way between Pélon and Sandor.

Every face in the building looked out.

"Go inside Ma, I can handle it," Pélon said.

Sandor was not so polite. He had his fist ready for Pélon, but had no objection to using it on the boy's mother. That was a mistake, but not his first mistake.

He punched her in the face. She went flying, smacked the concrete with a sound of breaking bone, and lay still.

It was bad for Sandor that none of Pélon's brothers were around.

Pélon crouched over his mother and saw she was unconscious. And then it happened. That wire that was loose in Pélon's head came completely unglued.

Sandor didn't know who he was dealing with. He grabbed Pélon by the scruff of the neck and held him off the ground. One second he was laughing at the angry boy. The next, he was holding a whirling dervish of a spitting cat, all fists and teeth, and knees, and elbows. Even Mario had never seen anything like it. In the few seconds it took to run up the walk, Sandor was flat on his back for the last time. Sandor died screaming, "Get this fucking vampire off me!"

Mario pulled Pélon off, Pélon whose face was bloody because he had a mouthful of Sandor's neck.

Three ambulances came.

One took Pélon's mother to the hospital, one took Sandor to the morgue, and a third took Pélon away to who knows where. He didn't come right home to Mom that time. There was a month when he was in juvenile hall for murder, and another month of delays because Pélon's mom had been too broken up to go to court. But when they'd finally gone in front of the judge, dozens of witnesses stood up for Pélon, including

Mario, Honey, and Officer Dibble. It didn't hurt that Dibble had gotten pictures of Sandor's massive gorilla hands, and that Señor Chapo brought a picture he'd blown up of Sandor at the fair, taking up the whole picture, with Pelon's mother's big hair and tiny head barely inside the frame. He'd cropped Mario and Carmen out of the picture.

Mario found out at the trial that Pélon's mom's name was Iris. As far as he and Carson had been concerned, her name was Mom. It was the first he'd noticed she even had a name, though he'd known their last name was Contreras. Pélon's brothers, all much larger, wisely stayed away from the courtroom so the somewhat naive juvenile judge could see little Pélon and his petite mother in her body cast, her face a lingering green from the bruises. Her head, however, was undamaged. She had landed on her hair.

During the trial, Pélon became a neighborhood hero. Most of the corner girls thought it was romantic that Pélon had come to his mother's defense, or that his mother had come to his defense. The accounts of what happened got garbled. The story was told and retold, and with each telling, became more mythic. Nana, especially, thought Pélon was a good boy. She had a long history of mistrusting the law, which had let her down many times, as well as many of the girls under her wing. Dibble, who frequented the house visiting Honey for his weekly 'husband' lessons, assured her that he was going to do his best for Pélon. Worry and stress sent Nana to her bed on a Friday night, and there she stayed. Honey, who wasn't all that charitable or nice to anyone else, never left Nana's bedside. Nana thought Honey was a saint. Honey was no saint, but she was a hell of a good actress.

Mario did not normally discuss Nana's house in front of Aunt Carmen. He knew she helped the girls when they were in the family way, but he was well trained that the "decent" ladies of the neighborhood did not mingle with Nana and the corner girls. Mario felt certain Aunt Carmen would have a solution for Nana's illness too, but worried over how to bring it up. She worked a lot of hours, and she didn't spend any time hovering over him. He was probably spending more time at Nana's house than his aunt realized. But maybe not—there wasn't much that got past her.

It was on a Wednesday that he found the right moment. Aunt Carmen had worked too late to fix dinner, and brought home a casserole from the Mexican diner.

She put it in a ceramic dish, and heated it in the oven, as Mario set the table with three places. Señor Chapo had brought wine and ice cream.

"Any news on Pélon?" Señor Chapo asked.

"Dibble said he's doing ok," Mario said.

"Iris wants to come home. I stopped by the hospital and gave her some of this dish. You should see what they're feeding her," Aunt Carmen said, made a bitter face, and sipped her wine.

Mario waited until Chapo excused himself.

"You know Nana?" Mario said, "I hear she's sick."

Aunt Carmen got a thundercloud of an expression, but Mario had timed it perfectly, and Señor Chapo's return to the table put a screeching halt to the topic. Aunt Carmen would never discuss corner girls or Nana around Señor Chapo.

Thursday was always a slow night for Pixie. Most of the guys in the block lived from paycheck to paycheck; and by Thursday, the money had run out. Thus, Thursdays, Mario had a standing date with Pixie for the double feature at the movies. They waited until people had already gotten settled in, and always sat in a corner well away from anybody else. Pixie always distracted him, so Mario rarely remembered much of the movie. During Pélon's trial, he especially needed the escape.

In the intermission before the next showing, the lights came on. Mario liked how, when she wasn't wearing much of her usual "war paint," Pixie looked just like one of the girls in his class. She gave him a big smile, and told him that a young immigrant doctor had showed up at the house to make a house call on Nana. Mario was certain that visit was Aunt Carmen's doing. The doctor had chased Honey out of the room, and given her medicine. All of the girls had been very grateful, so grateful, the way Pixie told it, that he was still there, worn out from the girls' hospitality. "We might have to haul him home in a wheelbarrow," Pixie giggled. "You know what? I bet if Honey had her way, she would send him a bill. You know she wanted to make Hershey go away when she had her baby. Nana wouldn't hear of it."

Mario thought Hershey was a very nice girl. He brought popcorn and candy for his date.

"I'm so glad the doctor chased Honey out of the room," Pixie said, her mouth full of buttered popcorn. "I don't like Honey. She's bossy and mean, always trying to get Nana to make rules. If she did that, it wouldn't even be home any more."

Mario didn't think much of Pixie's anxiety. "I bet it will be okay," he said. "Nana's a tough old bird." He must have said or done the right thing because he didn't see all that much of the second movie either.

Pélon's crime was ruled self defense. He returned home like a king, with a red carpet and a new criminal entourage. He was quite proud of the whole incident, which had given him enough jail time to get the equivalent of a PhD in crime. His reputation was unhurt.

Some of Mario's friends were already dropping out of school, some of them forging their parents' names that gave them permission to drop out, some of them with their parents' blessings, and some of them were already doing time in juvenile hall. It was a miracle that Pélon wasn't in there doing time.

But Pélon was still a good friend. Not because Mario liked his ways, but because Pélon had always looked out for him, and they were still like brothers. Mario felt that if a person was good to him, he had to be good back. Mario wasn't perfect by any stretch of the imagination but there were things that he wouldn't do. He wouldn't mind screwing a teacher in the classroom storeroom when everybody was gone. (He'd sure imagined doing it with Mrs. Maloney often enough. He felt sure he'd be good at that.) He knew that you give your word to somebody, you don't just shoot them in the back or talk about them behind their back. You're friendly all the way. Mario would do just about anything for Pélon except go to a gang fight or join a gang. Anything else he would do. He would even lie for him, write him notes for school, especially first period English.

Mario encouraged his friends to work out. A couple of times, he even got Pélon in there to do some of the weights.

Pélon swore, "I don't want nothing to do with the karate shit." But he came in and started doing the weights. Not that it really helped him because Pélon gave up.

"This is too much work," Pélon complained, "I'd rather use a gun for self-defense."

Mario said, "Pélon, I know you don't mean that."

Pélon got up from the bench and looked at his friend. "You want to bet I don't mean that?"

"I know you don't want to rot in jail for the rest of your life. A gun is a sure-fire one way ticket."

Pélon didn't think too much. He sure didn't think about being kind. But he was loyal. Already he had a routine, and he was too busy doing the things he did best—giving people a bad time. Getting through school, barely.

For that matter, Mario was just barely getting through school too. He didn't like school. He didn't like any of those things you have to be good at to be good at school. He did have a good memory. And he still could spell really well, and had no problem reading. But he had trouble with everything else, like sitting in a seat for an hour at a time. He got along with his teachers, not because he had any special talents except for his mouth. He had a couple of women teachers. One of 'em he even had a worry about once in a while—a pretty blonde substitute. And he thought she liked him but then who knows. Some of the men teachers liked him too. They liked the way he talked. Every once in a while, they'd have a heart to heart with him. They'd tell him that he should settle down, work harder, put some effort in, go on to college. They warned him against following in Pélon's footsteps.

He liked Mrs. Maloney though he still hated English. He didn't want to be known as a teacher's pet, but her pet, maybe he would not have minded being, and neither would any boy in his class—or any male on the campus, for that matter. Sometimes she had him stand up and read aloud. That was no problem, though when he was done, he had no clue what he read. Usually he didn't pay much attention in class; he would just look at her legs. She had a great body for a teacher. She had a great body for anybody. And then midway through the year, during first period, she said something.

"I want to see you after school, Mario."

When she asked him to stay after school, he was pretty excited. It ruined him for the rest of the day, since hour after hour he imagined that when she wanted him to come to her after school, that she really wanted him.

In second period science class, he pictured going in after school with a gift, maybe a candy bar from one of the vending machines, and he accidentally let the Bunsen burner ignite the cord to the Venetian blinds. In third period history, he thought about how he would tell her she was the most beautiful teacher in the school. Dona thought he was making eyes at her and sent him a note asking if he wanted to meet her after school. During lunch he thought about how Mrs. Maloney would blush and bat her eyes like all the girls did when Mario gave them compliments. He'd ask about her husband and give her the chance to say how he didn't understand her, and how she was so lonely. In fifth period health class, he imagined how he would lean over her desk and kiss her and tell her how he wanted her too, how he would do anything for her. In sixth period gym, he was glad he was on the bench, because he imagined how she didn't resist him, how she would get up and kiss him on the mouth and give him the keys to her apartment. He was so wrapped up in his fantasies that he couldn't get in the shower. (Then they really would have teased him about how big he was.)

So he combed his hair. He took off his sweaty t-shirt, and put on a clean spare button down, leaving the buttons half undone. The second the bell rang, he headed straight for her classroom. He walked up to her desk, just like his fantasy, only there was a big stack of papers in the way. That minute she was grading papers, and she happened to be wearing the big round unfortunate glasses that made her look like an owl. He leaned over like he was going to kiss her and….

"Have a seat, Mario," she said crisply.

Mario didn't sit, but watched her adoringly.

"Is there something wrong with your eye?" she said, sounding worried.

He sat.

He felt awkward—his knees were all over the place on the small chair. Maybe he could get close so he could put his hand on her leg and she'd understand.

"Tell me about your husband," he said, in the deepest voice he could manage.

"What?" Mrs. Maloney said, setting her grade book aside, "I didn't understand you?"

Mario waited for her to confess her feelings. She waited for him to repeat himself. "I have this feeling, Mario…"

Here it comes, he thought, his heart racing.

"You're a nice boy, Mario, and one of my favorite students…"

Yes! he thought, he knew it. He'd known it all along. But she didn't grab him like Pixie did. She just kept talking.

"Mrs. Maloney, you're the most beautiful—what?" he said.

"…but if you keep on at this rate, you're going to flunk," she continued on, not hearing him. "If you don't do your work, I'm going to have to flunk you even though you're probably the smartest student I have ever had. If you could just use that brain of yours for fiction," she sighed, "and that mouth of yours."

She actually glanced at his mouth and looked a little guilty when she said that, but for Mario the moment of possibility was gone. He slumped back in his seat while she talked on about how important school was, and how if he would just put forth some effort and then go to college, he could do anything he wanted as a grown-up, even be a lawyer. She gave him a packet of work to do, and promised him that if he would just do it all, she'd give him enough extra credit so that he wouldn't flunk, and then he might still be able to get into college.

"College. I'm having enough trouble with what I got now. Who the hell is going to college?"

She didn't blink twice at his language, but shoved the papers at him. Woodenly he shoved them in his folder and promised that he'd turn them in. Pélon saw him come out of her room buttoning his shirt. Pélon had a good imagination. Within days it was all over school how Mrs. Maloney had ripped Mario's shirt off of him and had mad sex with him on her desk next to the potted begonia. Mario did nothing to correct that impression, either, though the only place it had happened was in Pélon's imagination.

He could think of a whole bunch of girls he knew wanting to attend college, and of course, a lot of his Japanese friends. But talking about it and doing it were two different matters. Mario knew he wasn't going to college, and he knew he wasn't going to talk about it, either. All Mario wanted was to get out of school, graduate like his aunt wanted him to. From then on, who knew what would happen. He just wanted to make a whole lot of money.

College. There was bound to be studying, more intense and even worse than what he was suffering through now. He imagined college as he saw it on television. Rich young men and women at parties, driving around in sports cars, running wild, living in dorms while their parents spent thousands of dollars to keep them there.

That would never happen to him, of that he was sure. Plus there was another four years to sit in chairs, listening to talking from people who really didn't know more than he did. Four years might as well be a hundred. At fourteen, he just needed to make money. He wasn't going to stick up a grocery store or bank. He knew about plenty of illegal things that were going on, but he wasn't going to do anything that got him into trouble, put him in Dibble's back seat, or that put him behind bars away from his aunt or that would gather his aunt any heartache. She had had enough heartache. He wasn't going to put more on her plate. So he kept being good, or at least tried to.

Aunt Carmen never caught him again with his pictures. He loved looking through those magazines with the women and men doing it, and though it taught him a lot, Pixie taught him a whole lot more. Aunt Carmen would never think to look for them in his closet, behind the removable board under the floor leading to the plumbing cleanout. Something was always in front of the tiny door. The magazines made him aware that maybe having such a big thing wasn't going to be so bad after all. Pixie's response was proof of that. Especially when he started realizing when it got hard it was really big. Pixie gave him all the practice he could handle and then some. And it was the craziest thing. When he was in Mrs. Maloney's class, he thought about Pixie. When he was with Pixie, he thought about Mrs. Maloney. When he was around neither of them, he thought of both of them. He thought about sex a lot.

He didn't let Cosmo know he was fooling around. Cosmo was a real character. He preached you couldn't smoke and be a part of his class. But he took breaks—smoke breaks—when his class worked out in his studio. He didn't have to teach all the time; he gave a couple of his best students free lessons for leading a class. These days, he sometimes had two classes going on at once. He didn't want to flood the inside air with the tobacco smoke, although he did smoke inside when he wanted to, and when there weren't students watching. If you really smelled, it wasn't just a sweaty smell that was there. It was a cigarette smell.

Sometimes the classes would hang in little groups, and talk about the unjustness of it all.

"Man, if he smells cigarette on your breath, you have problems. You have to do 200 or 300 pushups."

Tortuga was ticked off from the week before. He'd showed up at a class after bumming a cigarette—and the two dollars for the class—from Mario. Cosmo smelled the smoke on him, excluded him from class that day and he'd still had to fork over those two bucks. He was still pissed off over it. Maybe he didn't mind missing the class that much, but having to pay anyway—that got on his nerves. Mario wondered how Tortuga would have felt if he knew Cosmo turned around and gave the two dollars right back to Mario. Cosmo was strict about kids smoking or being late, and all of the Japanese kids forfeited their lesson for breaking his rules. All of them but not Mario. Cosmo didn't check Mario, and that was a good thing since Mario smoked. He took some of the money he made and bought cigarettes, or sometimes had somebody buy them for him. Then he started sweet talking the daughters of one of the market owners so it was no big deal getting cigarettes. It's hard to say exactly when the drinking started. There were always older boys hanging around with their quarts. When some of Mario's friends started drinking beer, so did Mario. It was no big deal getting beer. He didn't even have to get anybody to buy it for him. That's just the way it was. The big thing was buying quarts of beer in bottles, and the thing was to see how much you could drink. He only drank beer. He didn't know anything about liquor. Everybody drank beer.

One time when Mario came home, he didn't think he was drunk. Aunt Carmen had fixed dinner, and he was late. He meant to apologize to her for being late, but instead he just started laughing.

She was sitting there alone at their dinner table, her plate untouched because she always waited for him. She was sitting there watching him like a saint, with her hands crossed in her lap. Even her water glass was untouched.

He was laughing. He couldn't stop. He thought that was okay—he was just having a good time.

His aunt got up from the table. Very quietly she put away the food, the dishes. She stood at the sink for a long time, washing dishes, with her back to him, while he was still laughing in the living room. She dried the dishes, and she dried her hands, then crossed the room.

He didn't think anything. He should have been thinking something, but he was still feeling silly, still laughing. His aunt crossed the room and hugged him. That almost made him sober up, but he was still laughing a little until he realized she was crying. But he was standing there in the middle of their apartment, him laughing her crying. She cried. And she cried some more. She broke down and she cried cried cried, and was still crying later when she put him to bed, and tucked him in like she used to when he was a little kid.

When he finally got up the next day, it was a Saturday, so she wasn't working. His auntie met his gaze when he walked into the kitchen. She didn't condemn him. Her silence was harder on him than anything she could have said. He came into the kitchen, the heart of their little home, and he was glad to see she hadn't fixed him food. He was already queasy. He couldn't have faced his usual full plate. Mario felt bad. Boy did he have a hangover. But it wasn't the hangover that made him hurt. He confessed all in a rush, dying for her forgiveness.

"Auntie I'm so sorry I did that, I...I...I...I've really really never done it before."

He was lying. He hated to lie to Aunt Carmen. Carson lied all the time, to everyone, and lied so much he couldn't keep track of the lies. But while Mario liked making stuff up, he didn't try to pass it off as real. He imagined things and tried to make them happen, whether it was a goal of a certain number of clients, or a new adventure with Pixie. Even worse, he hated to lie to his aunt. He didn't consider sneaking around with his magazines the same as lies, because those were secrets for her own good, but it wasn't the same. Here lies were coming out of his mouth. He was lying. Even though he knew it wasn't fair, he almost blamed her for it too, because she was the one who had such expectations of him. If she didn't expect so much, he wouldn't have to lie.

And she shrugged, and said, "All I want is the best for you Mario. You're such a young boy. I can't imagine that somebody would be so bad to give you something to drink knowing you're just a minor. If you drink at fourteen, Mario, if you start, it's going to make you a drunk. If you become a drunk, you'll never become anybody. You'll live and die and just be a drunk nobody with a beer belly and a headache."

All this made him feel a million times worse.

He wanted to shrug and ask "What else am I going to become anyway? Am I going to be a Cosmo giving lessons someplace, maybe in West Los Angeles so I can get more business?" He couldn't say that to her. He felt terrible. And he stood tall in the tiny kitchen he'd grown up in, and he cried and she cried. He hugged her back and wondered what he was going to make of his life.

She didn't ask him to promise that he would stay away from liquor. So he didn't volunteer it.

He decided to be careful from now on because he saw something he didn't think could ever happen. He had seen Aunt Carmen really break down. Seeing him drunk just broke her heart.

He realized there was a lot of reality his aunt couldn't deal with. That included drinking beer, looking at fuck mags, pulling girls' skirts up and squeezing their bums. She had cared for him his whole life. He was a man now, and it was his job to protect her. Mario decided that his aunt would never learn about any ugliness in his life.

He was more careful after that.

There was drinking, and there was drunk. At fourteen, he had no craving. He was just trying to fit in. So that's what Mario did. He drank enough to fit in, but not enough to impress anybody. His friends that he'd run with after school, they'd go over to Hollenbeck Park and drink a quart. It was all about "Eh, who's springing for the quarts?"

Pélon, where he got his money, he just intimidated people. By the time he was fifteen, he stayed away from the Japanese. They were little but now they weren't defenseless. They were taking self defense classes, some of them for four years now. Pélon didn't blame Mario; Pélon had been part of making them go to Mario to learn self defense. But of the ones not taking classes, he intimidated whoever he could. He took money from them. A quarter, fifty cents, a dollar, whatever he could get. He got it here, he got it there, he pushed his way through, and then he'd go to buy the beer. That was Pélon.

That wasn't Mario. Sure, Mario respected the power that was Pélon. Pélon was still like Ella, like that old saw, it wasn't the size of the dog, it was the size of the fight in the dog. Mario was still Hermanito, the big dog who walked softly where ever he wanted to, who only barked when he meant it, and never had to bite. Mario didn't want to be someone that got something because he held them up, or because he pushed them or because he intimidated them with his size, or with the knowledge he had in karate. The way he was buff now, after four years of Cosmo working him twice as hard as he worked everybody else, he could have kicked some real ass. He could have written the book on intimidation. He could have intimidated all of those shrimps he went to school with. Hell, they were already intimidated, and he'd never done anything. One thing everybody saw for sure is that Pélon left him alone, and that had to mean there was grit to Mario that they couldn't even imagine.

It's true there had been a confrontation but not one in the public eye.

It had happened at Pélon's during the Friday night poker game. It was the usual crowd playing: six of the moms including Aunt Carmen and Iris, and, of course Señor Chapo who wasn't a mom but who always sat in.

Four of Pélon's brothers were home. They had brought two of the corner girls, but Candy and Lemondrop looked just like high school girls, except for the fake eyelashes, lipstick and eye shadow. In their high school girl clothes, that's what the poker game assumed, except for Aunt Carmen, who rolled her eyes and kept her mouth shut. No high school girls had dressed like that in her lifetime. Anyway, they were paying more attention to their cards than what was going on with the kids in the den, even though it was just at the other end of the room.

The boys had gotten a television from somewhere, one in a big wooden cabinet, and they set it up in the corner across from two couches and a twin bed mattress on the floor under a sheet. The TV cabinet was missing a leg, but it was propped up on a cement block that was more stable than the wooden legs anyway. Señor Chapo looked over once or twice and might have guessed the truth about Candy and Lemon Drop, but he wasn't saying. The brothers who weren't sitting to look up the girls skirts were crouched around the TV and monkeying with the bent hanger antenna and knobs trying to find a channel with the game on it. Carson and Pélon were parked on opposite arms of one of the sofas, which was easier than muscling their shoulders between the rest of the Contreras brothers as they trickled in the room. Mario had walked in, almost innocently into the whole thing, though it was really Señor Chapo's fault.

Señor Chapo played a card, and asked Iris "So, why did you call him Pélon?" just before Mario came through the door. He hadn't even heard the question.

But he heard when Iris said, "Because he was the sweetest little bald baby. All my boys were hairy like gorillas, but he didn't have any hair to speak of until he was two years old, and even then we didn't think he'd ever have any."

Mario, startled, heard that answer, and said, "Who, Pélon?" and laughed. He couldn't help it. There was something kind of affectionate and funny the way Pélon's mom talked about her hairless little baby boy. The nickname for little Pélon had never made sense to him. Now it did.

The room fell to instant silence, except for the static from the TV and Mario's heaving laughter.

Pélon roared. He launched himself, like a projectile, on Mario.

It was the first time in years he'd gone after Mario. Even taken by surprise, all Mario did is take a step, and turn himself at an angle. Pélon flipped harmlessly on to the mattress, wedged between Lemon Drop and Candy's barely covered bottoms. Mario had his foot on Pélon's throat. Mario hunkered down, dug his fingers into the huge curly mass of hair on the smaller boy's head, and tugged. He ignored the crazed fight in Pélon's face, and after a second, said, "Hey, Baldy, can we trade places?"

Pélon realized where he was, and like any teenaged boy caught in a perfect fantasy, in a jiffy had his hands full of girl bottoms. As for the girls, they were both screaming with laughter. Mario moved his foot off Pélon's neck. Situation diffused. The only ones annoyed were the two brothers who had brought Lemon Drop and Candy.

Mario was half past fourteen. It was late in the day. The studio was empty except for Cosmo where he sat at his little desk, in one corner, and Mario in the opposite corner where he had the bench and weights.

"I should move. Business is good," Cosmo mumbled.

"If business is that good, move," Mario said, between lifts.

"I need a bigger place," Cosmo said. He shuffled papers around on his desk.

"So move," Mario said. It wasn't the first time they'd gone through this. He wasn't even paying that much attention to the conversation.

"Why should I pay more rent? Just because I need a bigger place."

"So move someplace cheap. Move someplace across town and buy me a car so I can get there." Mario was only half kidding. He wanted a car so bad he could taste it, but there was no way to save any money. His aunt told him they used every cent that they made just to make ends meet. His aunt was making more money, and so was he. But her bosses just took out more deductions because now she was on the payroll. And everything was getting more expensive.

"I can stay here. All I need to do is work later hours and have bigger groups and double up on classes."

"As long as the groups come in, they can do their lessons, and I get paid, I don't care if the classes are here, in Hollenbeck Park, or the lady's john at the Bradbury Building," Mario said. So much for talking Cosmo into getting him a car. But Mario had time. He was just fourteen and a half. He had another year and a half to work on him.

Mario started on his sit ups. Sometime between the 50th and 100th rep, a man came in. He had a familiar face, but everybody had a familiar face on Brooklyn Avenue. He didn't look like he was the type to sign up for karate lessons. He wore a tie, but it was just hanging on him, and he was wearing a sport coat. It wasn't what people wore to do karate, but what did Mario know about dressing?

The man with the familiar face was already inside, but he went back and shut the door hard enough to jingle the bell. Cosmo looked up. He got up from his desk, came over to him.

"Harry, how are you?" They shook hands. "How ya been? You haven't come over in so long."

And Harry said, "Yeah, whenever I peek in, you're really busy."

Cosmo went into it and said, "You see that kid over there? Mario, come over here for a minute. Meet our neighbor. This is Harry Schwartz, the lawyer from across the street."

Mario took his big, tall, buff body and moved over to the center of the room where they were. He shook hands with the man and checked out his shoes. Shiny shoes. Aunt Carmen always said you could tell a man by his shoes. This man's shoes were very shiny. Mario kept his shoes really shiny too. Mario was without his t-shirt, but the shoes he had on were as shiny as the stranger's shoes were.

Harry asked, "So how many sit ups was that?"

Mario reached for a towel and swiped it across his face. "I lost count around 200."

Harry whistled. "I hear you're the one responsible for all of this action here with Cosmo."

"He is just the best salesperson ever, just unbelievable. There were days that I really wanted to just close up shop, except that I had a lease here I had to live with. Now I wish I had a bigger place."

"That should be easy to handle. If business is that good, move," Harry said.

Mario snorted.

Cosmo just laughed.

Harry said, "What's so funny?"

Mario shuffled back toward the weights. It was the middle of summer. He had a little bit of sweat running down his back, and stopped for a minute in front of the box fan for some relief from the heat. He took a quick step around the room, rolled up all the mats, and did a quick but thorough swipe with the dust mop.

"That last class didn't put up their mats."

The floors gleamed, but they didn't take much maintenance. Mario went back to the fan.

"They get lazy when you're here," Cosmo said.

Harry looked serious. He looked downright thoughtful. "You should come across the street and talk to me, Mario, unless you have a lot of business with Cosmo here. Who knows? Maybe I could use your services too."

And Mario said, "My services? You're a lawyer. What do I know about law? All I need to do is find people who need help to defend themselves."

"What do you think the law is if not a little help for people defending themselves?" Harry said, "Anyway, you could come in, maybe clean the office, get a look around."

"Yeah, that would be great except that you know, that's not the kind of work I like to do, but if that's all you're looking for, I could send you one of my friends who probably could use a job. I'm not looking for a job to sweep up anything, you know?"

Cosmo laughed and said, "Harry, he's a salesman. This kid is a salesman. I wish he could go to college and do something. Maybe become a lawyer."

"A lawyer! I can't wait until I get out of school. No more school." Graduation was still a couple of years away. How hard it was for him with some of the classes he had. "I wish everyone would get off my back about college."

Harry Schwartz said, "Come over. I'm serious. I'd like to talk to you. How old are you?"

"Fourteen. Fourteen and a half." Mario was already shaving.

Harry looked surprised. "You look older."

Mario did go see him, the very next day.

Like everything else on Brooklyn Avenue, the office was a store front. The plate glass window sported painted glass that said Harry Schwartz, Attorney At Law. The single door led to the open carpeted reception area with a desk where his legal secretary/receptionist worked. The building smelled old. It had been there a long time. In the back of the space there was a bathroom. Next to the bathroom, out of sight from the hallway there was a counter up against a wall where they kept a coffee maker and a kettle to warm water for tea. There was an old kitchen sink made of metal as well. The reception room out front was small and full of old chairs.

A secretary, who wasn't cute at all and was probably a hundred years old was sitting at a desk that was two hundred years old. She was nice, though, and greeted Mario with a big smile, a mouthful of yellow teeth and a friendly smack of chewing gum.

"Oh, you're the young man from across the street. I've seen you posting flyers about town."

"Yeah." Mario hesitated, not quite knowing what to do, then reached out and grabbed her hand, and shook it, maybe a little too determinedly. He was careful not to squeeze her hand though, it looked as though it might break.

"Mr. Schwartz is expecting you. Go on in."

So Mario walked into his office.

Harry was there, sitting behind a shabby desk mounded with a bunch of junk, a huge pile of stuff on top of that enormous desk. Behind him a credenza matched his desk, but it was so piled with file folders, the top could have been made of strawberry jelly and no one would have noticed. Stacks of typed pages almost to the ceiling were perched at either side of the desk. The files were piled so high that Mario saw Harry though an opening between stacks, and Harry had to stand and crane his neck to see Mario's entrance. The ancient, dusty light fixture centered in the ceiling was a beautiful piece from another century that did give enough light for the office, or would have if the stacks of paper had not cast eerie shadows. On the desk was a lamp, and behind him was another lamp over the credenza. Three worn upholstered chairs across from him were where clients sat. Harry sat back down, his sleeves rolled up as if he'd been up to his elbows in paper, instead of it being over his head. His jacket was hanging across the back of an office chair. Today he didn't have on a tie, and his collar was open. Mario wanted to look at his shoes to see if they were the shined ones.

They weren't.

"Have a seat," Harry said.

Mario sat, and craned his neck to see. He scooched the chair over for a better view.

"You know, I been here for over 20 years. I have a clientele. I do wills. I do leases. I settle disputes. I don't have to go to court much. Most of this is just paperwork. I tender my services mostly to Jewish people."

Mario shifted in the chair. It was old, and creaky, and too low for him. He wasn't exactly fidgeting but there was nowhere for him to put his legs.

"Every once in a while, I get a Latin in here. You know, or somebody from the projects down the way. But that's really seldom."

"So if you got business, what is it you're looking for?"

"There's a lot of money in automobile accidents."

"Automobile accidents? They happen all of the time. What's the deal?"

He said, "Well, you see, whoever is at fault, if they have insurance, we send the person to the doctor. When the doctor gives me a bill, I go to the insurance company, the responsible party and I collect some money. I take a third of whatever we collect. It's just that simple."

This was completely new to Mario. Mario saw wrecks all the time. It perked his interest.

"Cosmo told me about you," Harry said. "The truth is, I talked to Cosmo about you even before yesterday. He is ecstatic with what you did for him. How you got your friends over there. How you put up signs. How you had business cards made up. You've come a long way. I would sure like to have you do some work for me. Bring me in some of that business. This other work that I've done for so many years is crap. We have a chance to make more money. Real money, with these accident cases."

"Well, you say you represent all the Jews around here. Don't they have any accidents?"

"They do, they do but you know, most of my clients are in the neighborhoods here, sixty or seventy years old, and going ten miles per hour. I don't want to say they're too honest, but if they're not really bleeding or really injured, they're not going to make a case, they're not going to make a claim."

"So, what you're saying is that a person doesn't have to be bleeding or have a broken arm or anything to make a case."

"Of course not! There's whiplash. If somebody rear-ends you, your neck starts to hurt, your body starts to hurt. All your muscles tense up on impact, and sometimes there is a lot of internal pain. You start losing sleep at night, so you go to a friendly doctor somewhere here in East Los Angeles. You go there every day, every other day. At some point the doctor says you're ok. He gives me a bill. Depending on the size of the bill, say the bill is two hundred dollars for the treatment—"

"Two hundred dollars!"

"Yeah, let's just say it's two hundred. Chances are I'm going to collect six hundred dollars. I keep a third which is two hundred, we pay the doctor his two hundred, and we give the client two hundred. It works that way."

Even with Mario's math being as screwed up as it was, he could understand. He was talking about the case being worth about three times the amount of the doctor's fees.

"So what happens to the car. Maybe they have more damage than two hundred."

He laughed. "You're a smart kid. That doesn't count the property damage."

He had seen plenty of accidents; he lived on a busy street. In bad traffic, weather or construction, sometimes more than one a day. Some intersections were just prone to collisions.

Mario remembered accidents that occurred on Chicago and 4th where he lived, across the street from the church. There were always people getting run over there. And there was a crosswalk, only everybody came on it fast. Drivers zoomed through the signal. He recalled seeing somebody lying out on the pavement while the police and ambulance people hovered over them. He thought that person died because they covered him up and took him away.

"You know I still don't understand how I can help you. But I might be able to figure out a way. It looks like you're going to make $200 from what you tell me on your case where a person is not bleeding. What about a big case where a person goes to the hospital or even dies. What's in it for me? What am I going to get? I know what I get from Cosmo when I bring somebody. "

Harry Schwartz put on a fatherly smile, "What do you make from Cosmo?"

Mario told him. "Mr. Schwartz that's none of your business. I think we're here to talk about what you're willing to pay me if I can get lucky and bring you any business. Okay? And I don't want to talk about any percentage, either. I'm not that good with numbers. I like to think of things as flat fees."

"I'm sure we will come to an agreement."

"Okay, but I'm telling you, I need to find something where I can make plenty because I need to buy a car. I got obligations at home. It's going to have to be a good deal for me. Because I gotta go out and invent a way to get your business."

"You don't have to invent. You got body shops out there, up and down on Olympic Boulevard and on Atlantic Boulevard. They all have these cases. The tow trucks at Hollenbeck Towing on Boyle, they're first on the scene. Maybe you can figure a way to get friendly with them. They're working on cases. If you can get to them soon enough, maybe you can talk to the people. You're a tall kid, good looking kid, you look old for your age. And you can talk. Check out Hollenbeck Towing, over on Boyle. There's a lot of ways for you to get cases. You get to know people at the emergency room. People in ambulance services. Police."

Mario mulled over what he said. "You know Mr. Schwartz . . ."

"Call me Harry," Harry said.

"Harry, if it is that simple, why aren't you doing it?"

So Harry laughed, "Son, look, I'm a lawyer. Lawyers can't solicit business like that."

"Solicit. Like the corner girls." Mario made a face.

"Not exactly. It just means to drum up business—approach people. Solicit. If I went to a body shop and handed out my business card and told them to call me every time there was an accident, I could get into trouble. You could do the same thing on your own and not be in trouble."

"What kind of trouble? Like go to jail?"

"No, but I gotta answer to something called the state bar. They have rules, call them ethics. Take my word for it. I can't do it. As a lawyer, I can't do it."

"So, what? You want me to go to jail? Do I need to answer to somebody like the state bar?"

Once again, the fatherly chuckle. "No, Mario, not at all. I'm not even sure this will work but I have this feeling that once you get an angle on it, you would be good at this. You're smart enough. I can't believe talking to you that you're not even fifteen years old yet."

"Yeah, well, I wish I were older. I wish I could drive."

"Go out there, think about it. Find a way. The first time you bring me a case, then we'll talk about what you get. And to keep you thinking about it," Harry reached into his pocket and pulled out a wad of bills. He said, "I'm not a rich man. But I have a nice little practice here. Everybody pays me cash. So I always have cash laying around. Here's a hundred bucks for you."

That was a lot of money. Mario looked at that hundred dollar bill. He couldn't remember ever holding one of those things.

"Why would you want to give me that?"

"Because I want you to really think about how you can help me. I have a feeling that you can."

"And what if I can't help you? Do I need to give you the hundred back?"

Harry laughed. "No son, you don't have to give it back. Consider it a gift."

"What am I going to tell my aunt when she sees this hundred dollar bill?"

"Tell her you got it from me. Tell her that I want you to come work for me. We're not quite sure what you're going to be doing for me yet."

"She won't believe you paid me for nothing."

"Tell her it's an advance. She knows what an advance is, I'm sure."

"Ok, I'll find something to tell her. Let me go think about this."

Harry reached across his desk for a box of business cards. He took out a small handful, held them out, and said, "Look, here are my business cards. Pass 'em out. Think of something to say. One thing though, you can't tell them that I'm paying you any money. You can't tell people that, I'll get in trouble. If anybody ever questions me on who gave out this card, I'm not going to tell them where it came from."

By now Mario was really confused, but he kind of understood that a lawyer can't go out and solicit cases. The lawyer could pay him for something, but not call it soliciting.

"Are you saying to me that because I'm not a lawyer, I can solicit cases?"

"It is like this. You can refer cases to me, all day long. You just can't tell anybody that I'm paying you to do it."

"I don't get the distinction, but let me go work on it. Give me those cards."

Mario glanced at the cards and thought of something.

"Wait a minute, wait a minute, there's something wrong here. My business cards with Cosmo have my name on them. If people come in here because I pass out your business card, how are you going to know that I sent them? How am I going to get paid?"

Harry said, "I don't know if I can get you business cards with a law firm name, let me think about it. Let's just see what you can do. Okay? The business card won't be a problem. Just go out and help me like you did Cosmo. Okay?"

Mario took that hundred dollars. Put it in his pocket. He just couldn't believe he had a hundred dollars all in one little bill.

Leaving the lawyer's office, his hundred dollars was burning a hole in his pocket. He wanted to run catty-corner across the street to Cosmo's, like always. He could just feel Harry and his secretary watching him through the window, not that it mattered whether or not they watched him. He wanted to tell Cosmo about the meeting.

He usually didn't use the crosswalk. If they're gonna run over you, they're gonna run over you. He thought about that person who'd been run over on 4th and Chicago where he'd lived, and the lawyer watching, and took the crosswalk.

Cosmo was just finishing up a class. Mario didn't disturb him. He went over to the weights and worked out a little bit, then stood by the door with his arms crossed. He could tell Cosmo was curious about what had happened between Harry and him. He stood by the door until all the mats were rolled up, and the place was emptied out. Between classes, he knew he had an hour to chat before more students claimed Cosmo's attention. Cosmo walked over to his desk and started filling out the wall chart of his next week's classes.

"Hey man," Mario said, sitting cross legged on the floor by Cosmo's desk.

"What are you doing sitting still down there? Why aren't you doing sit ups?"

Mario made a face, but pulled over a mat, moved on over to it, and started on the sit ups.

In between the up and the down, he said to Cosmo, "Look at this, man. Is Harry for real, or what?" Without missing a beat, Mario pulled out the hundred dollar bill and waved it around.

Cosmo cracked a big smile. He made a little move that, if he'd been a dancing man, would have been a two-step. Not that Cosmo was a dancing man. He said, "You mean you already got him some business? Good for you!"

"No! The guy just dug into his pocket and gave me a hundred dollar bill. I mean...what if I get him a lot of business, is he going to run out of money?" Mario put the bill back in his pocket.

"I don't know what kind of business you're going to get him. But I doubt very seriously that Harry is going to run out of money. That guy's got the first dollar he ever made."

"Yeah, I saw it on the wall."

Cosmo watched Mario critically, "Bend your knees a little more."

Mario thought about Harry's office.

"He sure didn't spend anything on decorating that office of his."

"It's just a figure of speech. I've known Harry for years. I've been here, what? seven, eight, nine years. He was the first person to come over and greet me. Of course, he could never take a lesson with me. He just didn't want to get involved in self-defense. So, what did you do? What did you talk about?"

Mario told him.

"Oh accident cases, oh, eh, I'm sure you'll find a way to get your people over there."

"My people?"

"You know what I mean. The people you go to school with. New clients. People in cars. People you can make a connection with that Harry can't. Who knows. Sounds good, whatever it is. You know I'll still take care of you as long as you continue bringing business, I can still give you something. It's not like I'm getting rid of you."

"You know I just thought of something. You probably put Harry up to this because you don't want to pay me that weekly amount no more."

"Don't be silly. That's not the case at all. You can count on this money. Don't stop the hustle because I can always use more business. You know, some fade out, some finish, some don't want to go any further. You know, I gotta have my income too, in order to afford everything, including you."

"I know, I was kidding. Do me a favor Cosmo. I don't want to take this hundred dollar bill home. I'm going to tell my aunt what happened, but I just don't want to take the hundred. By any chance you got enough change for that?"

He knew before he asked. Cosmo always had a wad of money. Everybody paid him cash. Those two dollar bills added up.

"I'm gonna have to give you a lot of ones."

"Oh, bullshit. Stick your hand in the other pocket. Give me big bills—give me some twenties and tens, okay?"

Cosmo changed the hundred dollar bill for him.

On his way home, Mario stopped at this little flower shop that never seemed to have any business. He bought his aunt a big bunch of flowers. If his aunt knew he spent that much on flowers, she'd probably choke him, or maybe start crying because he'd done something horrendously wrong. He felt like doing something for her and he didn't know what else to give her. He had them all wrapped up because he didn't want to walk through the neighborhood carrying flowers. As far as the neighborhood was concerned, he was just carrying a package. Still, he concentrated on getting home as quickly as possible so he could unwrap them and they wouldn't be hurt.

They didn't have any vases. He put the flowers into a pot and backed up to look at it. He poured in some water and stood back again, to get another view. He put the pot on the kitchen table, and tried to bunch the flowers together differently. It didn't help. He moved it to the counter. That didn't help either. He turned the pot so he couldn't see the handle. No better.

"Why didn't I maybe think of buying something to put 'em in? This looks terrible." He put the pot of flowers back on the kitchen table and tried adjusting one or two of them.

He was thinking about going back out and getting a vase when his aunt walked in. She saw the flowers right away.

The first thing that she said was "Where'd you get the flowers?"

"I got 'em for you, auntie."

"What did you do wrong?"

"Gee, Auntie, nothing. Why do you think I did something wrong?"

"People give flowers to apologize for what they did wrong."

"Auntie, I've done a whole lot you said was wrong, but I never got you flowers for it."

She thought for a minute. "You have a point. But you have done things before to butter me up. So, why are these flowers here?"

Mario hedged. "I want to talk to you while you're cooking dinner."

"That doesn't sound good." His aunt looked from him to the flowers, speculatively.

"No, not bad, I promise."

They were both standing, the dinette with the flowers, between them. Mario pulled out a chair and sat facing her.

"You know A

untie, you know I'm good at promoting and advertising."

"Well, you must be, you get paid every week. You get paid too much."

"What do you mean too much? If he can pay me that much, imagine how much he's making. But anyway, I have this, I don't know, I don't want to say something stuck-up, but I have this ability. So anyway…" His voice trailed off. Mario wondered how to continue.

His aunt stopped moving around the kitchen and looked at him, "So anyway what?"

"So anyway, there's a friend of Cosmo's who's across the street. He's a lawyer. And I met him the other day—yesterday, and I went to see him today. And he wants me to work for him. He wants me to promote for him too, get him business."

"How are you going to get a lawyer business? What kind of business?"

"Auntie, I don't know. But, I didn't know how I was going to get the people I got for Cosmo the last couple years either. Let me work on it, okay? I was just trying to share something with you. Don't start imagining things like I am doing something wrong."

He kept thinking of what Harry said about the ethics thing and the promotion thing. His aunt had never really asked how the arrangement with Cosmo worked; she probably wouldn't ask about this, either.

His aunt reached into the cabinet and pulled down some mixing bowls. She set them down on the counter, but she didn't start preparing anything. She fixed her eyes solemnly on Mario's face. She glanced toward the flowers, then back at him.

"It's a long story, I can't run it all by you, okay, but it involves people that have accident cases. There's accidents everywhere, he's gonna pay me for bringing in the people, if I can find some of those people after they wreck and before they hire a lawyer."

"But what does he do with the people?" She sounded perplexed.

"I don't know. Whatever he does, he's willing to pay for. He's a lawyer.

I'm sure he's not going to do anything wrong. If you have a problem with him, go talk to him like you did with Cosmo."

She might not do that now that he was going on fifteen. She trusted him.

"And Cosmo knows him?"

"Yeah, he's one of Cosmo's best friends. You know Cosmo's not going to hook me up with somebody who's gonna get me in trouble."

That made sense to her. "Well, that's good." Then a worried look crossed her face. "So are you gonna leave Cosmo? He's been awful good to you."

"Of course not. We need the money. If this works out, I gotta cut him a little bit of slack. I mean, there are weeks go by that I don't get any new business for him, but he still pays me a cut because the students I brought him are still paying for lessons. And I don't know how many more students he could handle. He has more than there's room for, now. I have no idea what I'll be able to do for this attorney. But anyway, here's the situation, auntie, he hands me a hundred dollar bill. I was gonna bring it home but I figured—I was afraid I might shock you."

"A hundred dollars! For what?"

"He gave it to me. He said to tell you it's an advance, and that you'd know what it is. Of course, I'm gonna give him something back for it—the people he wants. The ones who had accidents. I gotta make a deal with you though. For whatever I do with him, I'm gonna need a telephone. At least I have to have a phone where people can call me or I can call them. I'm not here all day, they gotta be able to call me after school, after I'm home. We need a telephone."

She didn't say anything. She pulled down a battered looking brass pot that had been hanging on the wall as long as Mario could remember. She pulled a scissors from the drawer, and snipped a few of the stems before dropping the flowers into the brass pot. At once, like a falling cat, the blossoms flexed and eased into a smooth arc of color, like a little floral horizon setting, like the setting sun, into the brass pot.

She added water.

"Wow," Mario said. He wondered how she'd known what to do to fix the flowers. The one person he'd known every minute of his fourteen and a half years and she had talents he knew nothing about. What else did he not know about her?

But Mario was developing into being a man of action rather than a philosopher. He didn't know what she'd done to fix the flowers, and unlike his younger self who asked questions, he was more concerned with results. And the result he saw was that she hadn't objected to his getting a phone. He counted out some money.

"Here auntie, here's eighty dollars of the hundred he gave me, I'm going to keep the rest—the flowers I bought—"

"Oh! You shouldn't have spent that money—"

"Auntie! Please! You deserve so much more than the flowers." He hesitated, feeling a little shy. "I know I don't show it like I should, but I love you."

"And it's not even Mother's Day," Carmen snapped back, but he could see her with the tears in her eyes. She was so emotional. She even cried in church.

"Auntie, look, for once, don't give me any trouble. Tell me we can get the phone. I'll pay for it, okay? I have no idea what it will cost, but I will pay for it. If not, we can disconnect it. Okay? We'll take it off, okay?"

He remembered when they'd repossessed the television set. "Sometimes if you don't pay, things go away anyway," he said. "I need this phone. I have some ideas, but I need a phone. I need a phone number. I don't want to use the attorney's phone number. I'm not there."

His auntie took the eighty dollars, and said, "I'll get the phone. Not because the flowers buttered me up. I'll get the phone because you didn't ask like a spoiled child, the way Tortuga asked his father for a motorcycle, or the way Dona asks for make up when there's nothing but rice and beans in the pantry after her mother had lost her job, and not the way Pélon and his brothers sit down every night expecting poor overworked Iris to feed them steak. I'll get the phone because you ask like a man, for a man's reasons—not a child's—and you pay your own way. I just hope the neighbors don't think we're getting uppity."

"They won't. They'll be over here all the time, using it."

"They will at that." She looked around. "I think it should go on that table. Maybe we should get a chair to go next to it." She pretended to sit, pretended to hear the ring, and pretended to pick it up. "Definitely need the chair."

Mario felt all choked up. "Auntie, I love you."

He got up and hugged her. It only made her crying worse. Sometimes he wished aunts came with a manual. Sometimes it was so hard to know how to act to please them. Finally, he said, still hugging, "I'm hungry, Auntie. Shall we splurge and go out to eat? Go celebrate?"

The suggestion was like a slap in her face. She bounced back, with her usual salt.

"What do you mean, eat out? We're eating here. What are you talking about? We have a refrigerator full of food."

She opened the refrigerator and started grabbing ingredients. Behind her back, Mario chuckled a little.

***

Barbara, Harry Schwartz's secretary, had been forewarned that Mario might get some phone calls, and that he would be calling in to get these calls. He asked her the magic question.

"Do you speak Spanish?"

"Only enough to get a message. I can't converse."

The next day, Mario returned to see Harry. The law office was deserted except for Harry, Mario and Barbara the secretary, chewing gum and typing away. Harry saw him through the open door and said, "Come in, come on in." The pile on Harry's desk hadn't noticeably changed. A different sport coat and different tie were draped over the same chair.

Mario kidded him. "I'm here to pick up another hundred dollars."

Harry looked startled, not sure at first that it was a joke, which made it a better joke. Which made Mario laugh too, at Harry's reaction. They both laughed, and that put Mario more at ease.

"Have a seat," Harry said. "I brought these from home a couple of years ago when my wife purchased a new living room set."

Mario sat in the too short chair.

"I have some ideas about seeing people. I don't even have a telephone yet, though they're putting it in. So if I pass out their cards, they're going to call you, you're not going to know that I had anything to do with somebody calling you."

Harry raised his hand and said "I will assume that it's yours—"

"I know, you'll assume that it's mine, but I'll have no way of knowing, nor will I be able to count."

"Let's try this," Harry said, "I've got some cards for you. My secretary has them. They're a different color, on different cardstock, ivory with black letters. When I see those cards, I'll know it's you."

Mario nodded. "And there's another thing. I need to know right now what I'm going to get for every person I bring you here that's had an accident—"

Harry quickly said, "The fact that they had an accident is not the entire story, Mario. They have to have had an accident. They have to be injured in some way, willing to go to a doctor even if it isn't visible injuries, and like I told you, depending on what their medical bills are, and depending on how much their property damage was, which is the amount to repair their car. Most important is whether or not it was their fault. If it was their fault, there's no deal. Another thing, if you get the person who's not at fault, but the person who hit them doesn't have insurance, it's no deal. So you need to consider those things."

Of course, all this information set Mario's brain spinning, and pumped him up with a whole batch of new questions.

"Okay, I understand. So if the person gets hit, it can't be their fault. So let's say that I find someone who has an accident, let's say that the person who hit 'em has insurance—"

"Oh, by the way, sometimes if the person you bring me has insurance on his car, and if the other person doesn't have it, there's something called uninsured motorist, that makes it the same as if the other person has insurance."

Mario blinked. "Ok, ok, we'll get into that the first time it comes up in a case. What I need to know is I bring you a case, the person's injured, the person who caused the accident has insurance, what do I get?"

"I could give you a percentage of the case."

"No, no, no, no, I can't deal with percentages. That doesn't work for me. I tried that with Cosmo. It doesn't work."

"In a way, I can't really give you a percentage. That's unethical."

"Unethical?"

"That's one of those things that can get you in trouble with the state bar."

"Oh, you mean like you said yesterday about soliciting?"

"Right. It's . . . if you're not a lawyer, I can't give you a percentage."

"Great, so we're on. We're in tune here. How much do I get?"

"It would depend on the size of the case."

Mario shook his head, wondering if he would ever get a straight answer.

"You really are a lawyer. Work with me here."

Harry laughed.

"I don't know about the size of the case. What do you mean, size of the case? You mean if the person is bleeding versus the person who is not bleeding?" Mario asked, answering his own question. He was only fourteen but didn't lack anything in the mouth department. He could snap. He could talk.

Harry nodded. "I'll give you fifty dollars for each person that you bring me."

"Fifty dollars," Mario said. He drawled out the words, and repeated them for good measure. "Fifty dollars" as if his ears couldn't quite hear what his mouth had just said. It was more than he expected. In an instant, his whole world changed. One single client per week would equal his aunt's entire income. It completely removed the ceiling. He thought of the hundreds of clients he'd sent to Cosmo. He felt dizzy and was glad he was sitting. He practically heard the choir of angels singing. Suddenly, there was no limit. Instantly, he was on new ground. He stood up. He sat back down again.

"What, you don't think that's enough?"

"Well, I'll never think it's enough," Mario said, though he was really afraid he was about to be offered less. "But I gotta figure you're going to make more than two hundred like you told me yesterday."

"Oh, that was just an average that I gave you, Mario, you can't hold me to that. There will be cases where I don't even make that much."

"True, but there'll be cases when you make a lot more."

Harry acknowledged with a nod, "Yes, you're right."

"Okay, so you give me fifty dollars. That's a good start. But here's my question. What if there's more than one person in the car?" Mario was watching Harry's face. He saw the surprise there.

"You're quick," Harry said. "Very quick. In the car that had no fault in the accident, when it was hit by somebody that has insurance, I'll give you fifty dollars for each injured person."

"Uh huh," Mario said, "I like that. I might even be able to save up for my car."

"If you're as good as I think you are, as good as Cosmo says you are, I think that by the time you...how old are you again?"

"Fourteen and a half and a couple of months. Fifteen in December."

"You can save your money, if you're smart, you'll be able to pay for the car in cash, by the time you're sixteen—if you're half as good as I think you are."

"There's just one thing, Harry, that you haven't told me. If there's more than one person in the car, and the car didn't cause the accident, but the other person doesn't have insurance, but the person I bring you has insurance, I still get fifty."

"That's correct. But the person you bring has to have uninsured motorist."

"Well okay, whatever that is. Now explain to me about insurance. What kind of insurance are you talking about? Is it the same kind of insurance that they taught us in school that you need to have in order to drive, or that you should have to drive a car?"

"That's right. So if you hit somebody, that's called liability insurance. The insurance company will pay for the harm that you cause a person up to a certain amount. We won't get into that, that's called limits. Then you also have insurance to cover your own car for damage. That's a different kind of insurance. That's called collision insurance. Okay? Then you have something called comprehensive insurance—"

"Wait, wait, wait! I don't need to know all that. I got the picture. You're saying they have to have car insurance, and if they don't have insurance, and they get hit by somebody that doesn't have insurance, they gotta have something called uninsured something or other, right?"

"That's right."

"Harry, what's my limit? What if I bring you so much business you don't have the money to pay me?"

"I am not going to run out of cash," Harry laughed. "You don't have to worry about that at all. I'm not Cosmo. If you brought me too much business, I won't get overworked. I would hire another lawyer. You would have to bring me an awful lot of business for that to happen, but if you did, I would bring in help."

"You better start looking for that other lawyer," Mario said. "I got it. I got it. I'm gonna go to work on this. Okay, I'll be back to you Harry. And that hundred dollars you gave to me yesterday, I want to thank you, okay? That'll be the first two people that I bring you, all right?"

"No, I gave you that."

"No, you don't have to gift me. I'm going to give you something in return. Okay? All right? I'll be back, I'll be back."

Mario stopped outside, interrupting the gum chewing secretary named Barbara. He waited as Barbara ruffled through her drawers looking for his cards. He could hear Harry in the office, on the phone. He could only be on the line with Cosmo.

"Where did you find this kid? You won't believe the questions he asks. Unbelievable. He's got a mind like a steel trap."

Barbara finally found his cards. Mario accepted the box. When he went out the door, he was whistling.

***

Monday after school, Pélon got Paco to drive them up and down Olympic Blvd. Paco was all of seventeen years old, a dropout with a gas station job. Mario didn't tell him exactly what he was looking for, except for body shops. So Paco drove his aging two door black and white Mercury up and down the streets, counting seven body shops where they re-paired cars for accidents. Anything that said body shop, he counted it. He didn't write down the names, he just counted. And then they went down another street and counted three more body shops, in among all the car dealers.

Mario gave Paco a five dollar bill, and said, "Hey man, thanks, here's for gas."

Pélon and he headed down 4th on foot to their neighborhood.

Pélon whispered, in case Mario was going to whisper something back that could get them in some serious shit, "What the fuck you doing, Man? What? Are you casing the joints? You gonna rob these people?"

Mario figured Pélon would have been pleased to hear about Mario being up to something dangerous. It would give them something more in common.

"No, I'm not gonna rob 'em."

"You're not gonna rob 'em. You are, you're gonna rob 'em." Eager like that, Pélon always reminded Mario of a not-really-angry Ella but in that territorial mood that bit unexpectedly.

"Getting them to send me business, is that robbing them? I'm telling you I'm not gonna rob 'em. Right away, you want to think of something crooked that ends up in jail. I promised Aunt Carmen, no crooked shit." Had Pélon even noticed that Mario wasn't going around shaking people down?

Pélon settled back, "Man, you getting pretty rowdy, the bigger you get. I'll kick your ass." He said it with his usual bravado, but not like he wanted to prove it. The truth was that ever since Mario flipped Pélon on his ass between the perfect and available asses of two corner girls, Pélon, who trusted no one, acted like he almost trusted Mario. It was almost as if Pélon didn't have to prove he was tougher than Mario.

Like always, Mario chuckled and said, "I know, you could kick my ass any day man, that's why I gotta be careful what I say to you. Right Pélon?"

"Right Mario."

They were like brothers, but so different. Mario stopped short of saying "I got your back." He didn't need a crystal ball to tell him Pélon was bound to get into trouble Mario couldn't get him out of.

The next day Mario was so anxious to get out of school, he almost ditched a couple of classes, but he waited it out. With his grades, he could not afford to skip. The second the bell rang, he ran to Harry's office.

Barbara said, "You're lucky. He just finished with somebody. He was in there for two hours."

"I need to see him." Mario was so impatient he could hardly sit still.

"Okay, go on in."

"Oh, you're back," Harry said as soon as Mario swung open the door, "Did you bring me anybody?"

"Harry, I got an idea. I want to run this whole thing by you, cause I don't even know if it's gonna work. But. I need you to give me two hundred dollars."

To Harry's credit, he didn't blink an eye. "Two hundred dollars. I gave you a hundred dollars the other day."

"I know. This is like when you start a business, you need something like, uh, capital."

"Yeah, sounds good, capital, I need capital. I'm gonna do something with the two hundred dollars—"

"What are you gonna do with it? Tell me, and I'll give you the money."

It all came out in a rush.

"I checked out the body shops. Just in a couple of neighborhoods. And I counted them, the body shops. So I'm gonna go over and have a talk with them. I'm gonna give out your cards and trust that you don't screw me. Okay? But when I go in there, and give them my spiel, what

I'm gonna do. I'm gonna say, 'Here's the first twenty for the first case you give me.' Kind of like you did with me with the hundred dollar bill. You got me all wound up, when you gave me a hundred dollars. So what I'm gonna do is I'm gonna offer them twenty dollars for every time they give me a phone call for something that works out for you. All right?"

The lawyer smiled. Big smile. He says, "I got the picture kid. You need seed money. Here's the two hundred dollars." He reached in his pocket, gave him two one hundred dollar bills. "You might try starting with five or ten, and see if they bite."

"Don't you have anything smaller than a hundred?"

But he took the bills.

***

Gonzales body shop was his first stop on Tuesday. Mario had Paco park a half a block away, then he walked in the body shop. He didn't want any gangbanger observed waiting for him. Outside of the building was a yard where cars were stored and under a wood overhang from the building were open stalls where the body men worked.

"Say, so who's the owner?" he asked, looking around.

The shop was an old warehouse, all open under one roof. Here mechanics worked on engines and the painter prepped the cars for spot painting or to do complete paint jobs. There was even a spray booth at one corner of the large building. This was a busy shop. There must have been fifteen cars there. Not all of them were being worked on simultaneously. But somebody was sanding; somebody was grinding; there was dust everywhere. He knew this wasn't going to be good for his clothes. Mario's shiny shoes were getting caked with grinding dust. It was noisy too. The man who seemed to be in charge was standing next to the office off by himself. He was dressed in real clothes, and all of the others had on matching coveralls with red stitched nametags. He must have been thirty-eight or thirty-nine, but he looked rugged, and his skin was a peachy red hue. His auntie had told him red faces like that come from too much drinking, and the guy did give off the faint scent of beer.

"Hi, my name is Mario. Mario Luna. Can I talk to you for a minute? Are you the owner?"

"Yeah," he said, "I'm the owner. I don't got no jobs, kid."

"No, I'm not here to talk about a job. I'm here to see if you want to make some money."

"I do nothing crooked, man. I don't buy anything that's hot. I don't sell anything that's hot, I just love what I do here, I make a good living. I don't want to—"

"Hey, wait a minute, you're jumping to conclusions. Do I look like a little gangbanger or something?" The guy looked him up and down.

"Well, you sure ain't little."

"That's right." Mario said, "I may be a kid to you, but I'm not that young either."

The man chuckled. "Okay, how can I help you?"

"Look. I work for a lawyer, okay, and we're looking for business. It's that simple. So you know, people come in here, they've had an accident, I mean, uh,—"

"Yeah, I get the picture," the man said right away. "Your lawyer, he's smart, he's sending you out instead of him coming over. I got lawyers that come over here and hit on me all the time like I'm the prettiest dame in the joint."

"What do you mean?"

"I'm the busiest body shop. They all want business. Lawyers all want business. What, you think this is new?"

"It's new to me," Mario admitted. "And what do they offer you?"

"Yeah, whatever it is, I never listen. I'll tell you why. See all this business I got in here?"

"Yeah, you're busy as hell." Mario had to yell over the noise of all the work the guy had.

"I get a lot of this, most of this from insurance companies. Okay? Insurance adjuster comes over, makes an estimate, he writes me a check made out to the person that owns the car, when I finish the job, the person endorses the check, and I got my money."

Mario made a mental note to look into another word. Two words. Adjuster. Insurance adjuster.

"And so? How does that affect what I'm trying to tell you?"

"Well, if all of a sudden, these cases started showing up at a lawyer's office, especially one lawyer, I know you probably don't work for more than one—"

"That's right, I don't." Now that he had started, it all came out in a rush. "I work for one of the best, he's been around for forty years. He's a good lawyer, he's around Brooklyn Avenue, his name is Harry Schwartz." Mario realized if he couldn't nail him, maybe he could get an education so he could go plow on Harry Schwartz for not giving him all the information he needed.

He said, "Tell me more about your situation."

Gonzales said, "I'm not a good prospect for you."

Mario's mind sponged up another word, prospect, prospect, prospect.

"But look, there's body shops up and down kid. Up and down here on Olympic, up and down on Whittier, up and down Atlantic. They're not as lucky as me, in other words, they do insurance work, but because the person that had the accident comes over, and they talk the people into doing the job when they get paid by the insurance company, or they leave their car because it's all banged up. The insurance company will come over. Insurance company will do everything in the world to try to take that job away from that body shop. Insurance company wants to send it to a place like me. They trust me. They like me."

"Yeah, I bet," Mario said glumly. "You probably take care of these 'insurance adjusters.'"

"Well, whether I do or don't, you can understand that I got a problem. I can't afford to get them pissed off at me. Sooner or later their bosses would find out. I'd lose a hell of a lot more than what any lawyer could pay me to refer any business."

Mario decided it was time to throw out the bait and see if Gonzales took it. "All right, well, I was gonna offer you a big twenty for every time you sent me something, man, you know, something that's good. I was even gonna lay the first twenty on you."

The man laughed. This time he really laughed. "Kid you got it together. That or that damn lawyer or whoever you're working with. He's really educated you."

"I was doing work long time before I met this lawyer. I've been promoting business for Brooklyn Karate Studio with Cosmo."

"Oh, the place with all the posters everywhere. I can't pull into a Safeway in this part of town without a Brooklyn Karate Studio flyer on my windshield."

"Brooklyn Karate Studio flyers, the posters, the cards, that's me."

"No kidding." He looked impressed. "Ok, so you're breaking out of that business? I got a little kid I'm thinking could use karate classes."

"No, I ain't breaking out of anything. My job is to promote business, to advertise. I can get you a deal with Cosmo for your kid." Mario pulled out one of his karate cards. "Day and weekend classes for adults, before and after school weekday classes for kids."

"Kid, about the lawyer, go try someone else. Good luck. There's lawyers who will give me fifty dollars to just send them a name." He took the card and squinted at it. "My kid is ten."

"A good age," Mario said. "I was ten when I started at karate. Now I go to tournaments and shit."

"You're a good kid. I like you. I don't even know you and I like you. Just keep your nose clean. Go hit 'em hard, man. I can tell you—go over here to Bustamante's. Right down the street. Tell him you talked to me. Tell him I told you to go over there. We're friendly, even though he's a jealous friend."

"Why's he jealous?"

"He's busy, but he's not as busy as I am. You'll see when you get there."

"I got it." Mario said, "All right, well thanks. Thanks a lot man." He shook his hand. "You're all right. You're real decent. I won't forget that. But you know, here's Harry Schwartz's business card. I'm just going to give you one. If you need me—I don't have a phone yet, I'm expecting to get one pretty soon, if you need me, want to talk to me, change your mind, or I can do you a favor, call that number. The secretary, Barbara is going to answer the phone. Just leave a message for Mario. All right? Here, I'll write it on the card." He scribbled down Mario.

"All right, kid, I'll take that. I wish I could help. I think I'd really like to do business with you. But it just won't work."

"Has it got something to do with the money? Because I'm not offering enough?"

"No kid, it has nothing to do with the money."

"Okay, well, I'm going over to Bustamante."

Gonzales was right. Bustamante's body shop wasn't as busy. Wasn't as big, either. It was an L shaped shop with a circular driveway and enough room for about nine cars in roofed stalls and outside storage for cars that were finished or waiting for repairs. The entire shop had a tall chain link fence with big double gates on the east and west side. There was no spray booth; the painter used one of the garage stalls or spot painted right out in the open. One of the mechanics was grinding away, and stopped what he was doing to look at Mario through his goggles. He waved him over.

"Hey, can you talk to me for a moment?" Mario said, "I need to find the owner."

"I am the owner. Beto Bustamante. What can I do for you?" He looked Mario over. "I ain't buying anything."

"Okay," Mario said. "What is it about me? It must be something about my face. Everybody thinks I'm selling something."

"You're not selling anything?"

Mario laughed. "Well, in a way."

Mario looked around the shop. He brushed off the top of his shoes, the back of his khaki pants. At least there wasn't any more loud grinding going on now. He could see a couple of employees, one over there in the paint department, another one stretching a frame or something underneath a car. Bustamante was waiting for him to continue. He wiped his hands on his coveralls, the same kind his employees were wearing.

"Look, I went next door, he told me to come over and talk to you. I work for a lawyer. I need to find some business, man."

"Okay, yeah, so he can't help you, 'cause he don't want to tarnish his precious name with the insurance companies, that son of a bitch."

Mario took a deep breath, and launched.

"Hey, man, look, I don't know what you got with him. He told me to come over here. He told me you were a real nice guy. He told me that if anybody could help me, it would be someone like you. 'Cause you don't depend on the insurance companies sending you business, that you do insurance business, but that its not like one of them one stop shops that he told me he is, over there." He gulped for air, having blurted out the whole spiel in one excited burst.

"You mean, he didn't badmouth me?"

"No, he didn't badmouth you. He says you're one of the nicest guys up and down Olympic."

Bustamante looked at him. Smiled. He knew his competition. He knew that man hadn't said that about him.

"Kid, how old are you? I know a con man when I see one."

"Hey, let's let that age part out of here, okay?" As usual, Mario got defensive when someone mentioned his age. "I go to school though. I can tell you that much all right, but I got a sick aunt at home. I'm the only one bringing in any money, I mean things are tough. So I gotta try what I gotta try. This lawyer Harry Schwartz, he's a real nice guy. I can't even talk about paying anything because he'll get in trouble. But look, let me just give you a card. I'm gonna have my cards pretty soon, I'm gonna be over here. I'm gonna give you a card with my name on it, and my phone number. You can call me after school and tell me if you've met somebody that had an accident. Then I'll go talk to 'em."

He switched to Spanish. "Do you speak Spanish?"

"Damn right I speak Spanish." Mario replied in kind.

The man immediately responded in Spanish, "Kid, you don't even have an accent. I'm impressed."

"Well, be impressed. I grew up talking both languages. So-why is that important?"

"Shit—everybody I get here is Mexican. They don't even speak English. Does this Harry Schwartz speak Spanish?"

"You know, I don't know." He thought about the woman out front. "It don't matter, I talk it. I'm the one that's gonna talk to the people. So can I interest you in doing something like that? You doing it with anybody else?"

"I ain't doing it with anybody. Lawyers promise to pay and then they don't pay. I tried it once."

"I ain't a lawyer. If I promise, I pay." Mario reached into his pocket. "I don't make very much even if a case is good, and if there's no case, I get nothing. But, okay, I'll tell you what, here's forty bucks." He pulled out a little wad of twenties. "Here's forty bucks. I was gonna use it to pay for two referrals." He handed over the cash. "Do me a favor. Take the forty dollars. If you want to screw me out of the forty, screw me out of the forty. All right? But I don't think you're gonna do that. So, what happens next, you owe me for two cases. I'll give you twenty dollars a case."

Bustamante didn't hesitate. He snatched up the cash. "Give me that phone number, man."

Mario wrote his name on Harry's business card.

"You call that woman Barbara, that's the lawyer's secretary. I'll be checking for my messages. You talk English to her, till I get somebody else on the phone. And then we'll play it by ear. Like I said, if you can't do it, I ain't sniveling. I ain't coming back to pick up my forty bucks."

Bustamante smiled. Slipped on his goggles. Said, "Kid, I'll be calling you."

***

Whenever Mario was really getting into his work, it seemed like Paco always had to go back to his job at the gas station. And he had no other ride. Mario had to settle for running his spiel by the rest of the body shops one at a time.

By Friday, Paco had delivered him every day after school to body shops on Olympic and Atlantic where he had first canvassed and even the one on Whittier Blvd. He didn't have enough money for them all. But he did clip some people that he had some good vibes about. He advanced them twenty dollars.

He'd advanced Bustamante forty because he was his first prospect, like a good luck charm. Harry gave Mario a roll of dimes for phone calls, and he'd hardly used any by the time the home telephone was finally installed.

Harry told Mario to use the rest of the dimes to get cards made. Mario could bring his referrals in, or they would play it by ear. They were into the second week, and no phone calls. Mario was getting antsy.

It was time to pay a visit to Richard at the printing shop. Richard still had the reputation of being a somewhat serious kid, one who wore glasses and read a lot. He did pretty well in English class too, thanks probably to long hours typesetting rather than any deliberate effort.

"I need to get this printed now," Mario announced.

Richard looked at him over the top of his glasses. By now, he'd printed several runs of cards for Mario. His karate card had been refined a bit— his choice of font, color, icon and style updated with each new run. "Oh, you leaving Cosmo?" Richard gave Mario a paper to fill out, to designate exactly what he wanted the card to say.

"No, but I need to have some cards that just have my name on them," Mario filled out the form and handed it back. He started looking through the heavy book of font styles and settled on a rather plain one.

"Okay," Richard agreed, making notes.

"Put Mario and underneath it say 'At Your Service.' And put down my phone number."

"You got a phone?" Richard sounded interested, "Moving up in the world. You want to put it here?" Richard pointed to one of the style pages.

"Yeah, that's good," Mario nodded. "I was going to put something else, but I don't think so."

"No pictures? No little icon?" Richard asked.

"I-What?"

"Icon. You know, like you have on the Cosmo stuff, karate."

"No, no, no, I don't want anything. I just want them to be able to call me. Then I hope that I'll be home to take the phone call."

Richard promised to have the cards done right away.

The next time he visited Harry's office, Mario mentioned his concern about not being able to get his calls when he was in school. Harry called Barbara in, and had her set Mario up with an answering service. That left

Mario with one last obstacle, as far as he was concerned. That problem, Mario thought, was transportation. He wasn't good at just waiting for something to happen. He felt he had to do something, so what he did is take the business cards that he had collected from all the people he gave money to, including Bustamante, and now that he had a telephone, he called them. He called in the order he'd seen them. Gonzales was first. There was no lawyer business, but he talked politely about Gonzales' son, a chubby red headed kid that Cosmo had probably worked five pounds off of on his first day. He'd dropped in at the karate studio, but had missed Gonzales son's class. The place was as quiet and serious as it could be with two classes going on at the same time. Cosmo was sitting at his desk in the corner, sipping tea.

"I see you're a man of leisure," Mario said.

Cosmo scoffed, pointing to a wall chart.

"I'm booked up for months," he said. "Two classes, every hour, every day of the week. On Sunday, we even have third class, a father-son class that works out in the alley behind the shop. We get a crowd."

"I just wanted to check in with you," Mario said, "I didn't want you to feel neglected."

"I'm far from neglected," Cosmo said. "I've got so much going on, I don't know where I'll even put another student. Unless I start doing a third class regularly in the alley. I've got the names of several potential part time karate teachers to lead classes if I wanted to stay home, but most of the time, I have a top notch student lead the class, and compensate them with free classes."

***

Mario dialed the next number on his list.

"Say, this is Mario. I haven't heard from you. I'm not leaning on you,

I'm just wondering, haven't you had any cases?"

Bustamante seemed pleased to hear from him.

"Oh, Mario, how are you? You know, we haven't had any estimates. Everything's been slow. I haven't seen anything that would interest you. But don't worry, man, I'm going to get in touch with you."

"I've got good news for you," Mario said, "I'll be by to give you some business cards with my name and my phone number. That way you can just call me direct."

"Give me that number," Mr. Bustamante said, "I'll call you."

"Okay, but ya gotta call after four thirty. That's when I'm at home for sure. If it's earlier, you'll just get the answering service."

Mr. Bustamante laughed under his breath, but all he said was, "I got it, I got the phone number."

Mario did this with five body shops where he had dropped off money. Between the body shops and Paco, he had spent the first two hundred dollars. Paco raised his cut to ten dollars; he said gas was expensive. That was bullshit. He knew Mario needed a ride and was sweating him. He knew Mario could not get around that quickly if he was riding a bus. Mario was reluctant to walk everywhere and show up all sweaty.

***

Carson had been nagging him for seed money.

"All I need is some cash. I have some business I can do, all I need is some cash to start me off."

"Is it legal?" Mario asked.

"Give a guy a break," Carson said. "It's me. What do you think?"

"This is what I think," Mario said, "I keep seeing everybody in the apartments, and every time they start up buying new furniture, or a new car, or wearing new clothes, or showing up with a new TV, next thing you know, they're getting bailed out of jail."

"You're always rolling in cash," Carson said, "I want to be rolling in cash too."

"Man, I know you," Mario said. "If your lips are moving, you're lying."

"I'd never lie to you," Carson said.

Mario laughed.

"I got enough trouble," Mario said. "Keeping things on the right side of the law. Just think what I could do with Pixie and Nana if I threw in with them. Just think what I could do with Pélon, if I started running with his gang. But I'm keeping it so honest, even my Aunt Carmen is sleeping easy."

"Just a C-note," Carson said. "That's all I need to start. I'll pay you back plus twenty bucks. I'll give it back to you in a week. I swear."

It hadn't been that long ago that a hundred dollars for Mario would have been about as close as the man on the moon; but he had more than that in his wallet now, every day, just for general purposes.

"As long as it wouldn't make Aunt Carmen stay up nights." Mario said, "You miss the payback date by so much as one minute, Carson, and I swear, I'll never loan you a penny again." Carson had never admitted whatever he was doing was illegal, but Mario guessed it had to be. Probably a drug deal. Just to make a point, he gave him a hundred ones. Luckily, Cosmo was still paying him for every time one of his students came in for a class, and that was twenty classes a day, every day of the week.

***

Friday when he was making a run in Paco's car, Carson accompanied him. Pélon was out doing his own thing. Mario looked him over critically before they left the sidewalk on Olympic. Mario knew he didn't look like a gangbanger, and when he took a real good look at Carson, Carson didn't really look like a gangbanger either. He was pretty straight except for the pomade hair. Everybody wore it except Mario. Mario didn't like that gummy shit on his hair, so he didn't use it. He just let it lay there naturally. He had it cut short. Carson was always dressed well enough, his shoes shiny, everything clean, and tucked in.

"Okay, let's do it," Mario said. "But you just keep your mouth shut, and listen."

Mario had him listen to his pitch to this body shop on Olympic. For once, Carson did as he was told.

"I'm Mario," he told the shop manager. "We talked on the phone. This is my buddy, Carson."

Mario explained Carson didn't have anything to do with the work but was learning the ropes.

Paco was parked in the car half a block away, because he looked like the gangbanger he was. It was far enough, but they could hear his radio from inside the shop, when the shop noise subsided to a dull roar. Paco's car looked like a gangbanger car: a low rider, a wildly painted Mercury. Mario didn't want to give the business the wrong impression. They took his card and twenty bucks.

As they walked back to the car, Carson was uncharacteristically quiet. Mario's developing business sense warned him something was coming.

Paco was up front alone, like a chauffeur, but he was happy enough with his radio. Paco didn't know much about keeping a low profile outside of their neighborhood. The radio was on so loud the car was vibrating. The boys both got in the back seat where they could talk, more or less.

"Man, what is the thing with this? I might be able to drum up some business for you."

"How you gonna go drum up some business for me?"

"I don't know—"

"You gonna go hit the body shops I already did the business with?"

"No, man—"

Paco squealed out into traffic, horn blaring. He yelled and swore at swerving cars like it was their fault he'd pulled in front of them. Mario and Carson ignored the swaying the screeching tires, the screaming, and kept talking business.

"Look, even Pélon waits for me in the car. You can't be messing with Paco taking you to places. He's a jerk but he's my ride. And you can't interfere in my territory. Got it?"

"Yeah, let me give it a shot."

"First of all, who you gonna see, who you gonna talk to?"

"I'll tell you what—when I find that out, I'm gonna ask you, and you can tell me what you want me to do."

"You heard the easy spiel. You heard what I just told this man. You saw him take the twenty bucks."

"Yeah man, but I ain't got twenty to give him."

"Well, tell me the area you're gonna go hit, these people. Show me the plan, and then we'll see."

Carson brightened up. He'd known all along where he was gonna start.

"Hey, remember Che?"

"Yeah, he's your relative, or something."

"Hey man, Che's a body man. He works for a body shop out on Washington, near Sears."

"Oh yeah? I ain't going out that way. You know, that's the Vago's territory, that ain't us. I wouldn't want to get knifed over there, by Vago's gang. Hey man, just don't go looking like a gangbanger, when you go over there. You'll end up dead."

Carson said, "How the fuck am I supposed to look? I got two pair of pants. I got two t-shirts. You know you heard me tell you this before. Ain't nothing else to wear."

"It ain't that, man, you look fine. You look fine. You look like I do. The big important thing is you can't go run over there with Pélon or anybody else Vago would recognize."

"Alright man. Let me try. I need to have something to do."

Mario remembered how Harry had said to grease the palms of hands you wanted to work. "Eh, you can make twenty-five dollars a pop. I'll give you twenty-five, but that's only for a case that's good. I'll explain what that means later."

Carson was quick. "I gotta give some of my twenty-five to who ever sends me the case. You don't think that Che is just gonna do this for nothing."

"Hey," Mario said. "Don't be so quick. Maybe he will. He's your fucking relative, right?" He didn't explain the part about the more people, the more money. He wasn't promising that much to Carson, because that would price him out of the gravy train.

"Yeah, you got a point, man. I'm gonna talk to him. Alright? This seems easy."

"Now, let me run it down to you what you can, and you can't do," Mario said, as if he'd been in this business for a long time, mentally sorting through all the things that Harry had told him that he would have to tell Carson.

"Okay, now look, you can never tell anybody that you're getting paid for the case. What you're doing, the lawyer says it's capping. See, so here's the story."

Mario raised his voice over the blare of the radio. The vehicle was bouncing down the street, squeaking. Bass notes in the music were making the windows rattle. Paco raced for the light, and lurched into a left turn, heaving Mario and Carson to the right side of the slick back seat. They untangled, and kept trying to talk.

"And then you got the insurance thing. Tell me about the adjuster. I feel like I should be taking notes," Carson said.

They went over a dip in the road. The car bounced, slinging everyone against the roof.

"I wonder if this is what popcorn feels like," Mario said.

Paco didn't respond. He was busy with his head out the window, craning backward toward a pretty girl who had walked past on the sidewalk.

Carson fidgeted and raised his voice too; he was getting stir crazy.

Paco wasn't paying any attention. He in his own world, and jamming to the radio which Mario asked him to turn down.

"Man, I can't think. And Carson can't hear me," Mario yelled. "All right, I'm paying you for this ride, so keep the noise down."

Paco said, "Fuck you," and gave him the finger. He dodged a couple of cars.

Mario leaned up, reached over the front seat, and turned it down himself.

Paco swore, but he saw the look in Mario's eye, and left it alone.

And Mario continued to counsel Carson.

***

"Harry if this works, it appears that I'm going to have a bunch of Mexican people coming in here. You're going to need someone to help Barbara. Somebody that will handle the phone."

Harry said, "That'll be the least of the worries, son. Get us the business, and we'll talk about expanding. For that matter, you could work here after school."

"If I worked here after school, who would be out at the body shops trying to get the business? That's not going to work, Harry."

Harry shrugged. He wanted to see action. "Go ahead kid. Go get 'em."

When Mario picked up the cards at the printer, Richard told him,

"You know, I read something that came into the shop. There's something now called a pager. A beeper."

This was news to Mario. "What's is it?"

"Doctors carry these things. Lawyers. So no matter where you are, within the area, I guess, it'll beep, and it'll show you the phone number of who wants you to call them back."

"No kidding. Can you find that article? Can you find it now so that I can find out about it? Do you know the company?"

"Oh, I don't know. I meant to set it aside for you but it got thrown out."

On his next trip to Harry's, he asked Harry about the beeper.

And Harry said, "Yeah, it's kind of a new thing. Service costs twenty dollars a month."

"Twenty bucks a month."

For Mario, that was too much. Maybe later when he had done some business.

"Could you look into the details for me? It's too much now but maybe when we're rolling."

Harry agreed. "Will do."

Even with his own phone number, up until now—it had been two weeks—nothing had come in. Carson had come in with nothing. The exchange people were real nice. He called in every day for messages, sometimes more than once, but they never had any.

Every time Mario saw Carson, Carson said, "I am working on my relative Che, but he ain't come through with nothing."

Mario called the body shops and started pestering them.

"Here's my new phone number," he told them, knowing he'd already called them before to give it to them. "And I'm going to be by and give you more cards."

He thought about Paco charging him five bucks, ten bucks every time he took him anywhere. That was getting too expensive. He couldn't afford much of that. He'd sit by the phone at home. He practically didn't go out, just to be there, waiting for a phone call. He decided he had better not push his luck and call the body shops a third time.

About a week after he got the phone installed at home, nothing had come in at home, the exchange, or the office. At least Barbara had said no calls had come in. Mario told himself sourly, what did she know? She chewed gum so loud, she probably couldn't hear the telephone.

So finally, he got a call from Bustamante, his forty dollars guy.

"I got a car in here," Bustamante said. "And the family was rear-ended. Let me give you the phone number. The girl's name is Teresa Sanchez. She's the driver."

"Thanks, Bustamante, I'll be in to see you."

"Hey kid, that's okay. I told you, I'd find something."

Mario braced himself to call his first client.

Teresa answered the phone in Spanish, "Who are you?"

"Just call me a friend. My name is Mario. We have a mutual friend, Bustamente. You know, I don't like to tell people I work for a lawyer but I do."

"I don't want a lawyer," she said in Spanish.

"Well, are you hurt? Are you hurting from the accident?"

"Yeah, we're hurt. Two of my kids also got slammed up. They're ok but they had some bloody noses. And my sister, and three of her kids."

"Boy, you guys were piled in. I can really help you," Mario said, thinking of getting paid for all those people in the car. "Let me come over and talk to you."

After a bit of coaxing, Teresa reluctantly gave him her address.

He took the bus to a stop that was four blocks from her house. When she let him in, he wondered where the husband was. Turned out that her husband didn't live with them. The sister was there too, and not in good shape. Teresa had a black and blue mark on her forehead.

"I hit my steering wheel there. I was lucky not to hit the windshield," she admitted.

"How about your sister, is she hurt too?"

Mario could see for himself that the sister's arm was swollen. She was lying on her back on a couch, with an ice pack, and a wet towel on her forehead. Every so often, she let out a little moan.

"She hit her arm." Teresa whispered, "It hurts her a lot. She has trouble moving her hand. But thank God it wasn't worse. The kids, they're gonna be fine."

"What did the doctor say?"

"We don't have the money for a doctor."

"I can get you money for the doctor. The lawyer, he doesn't cost you anything. He gets a third of the settlement. The settlement is what the insurance company pays. He gets the insurance company to pay for your car and your doctor bills, and your kids, and your sister and your sister's kids. Here is my card and here's the one of the lawyer. You can call me any time."

"And what if he doesn't collect anything?"

"If he doesn't collect anything, you don't have to pay him a dime."

"Are you sure they're not going to throw us out of the country?"

Mario threw his hands up. "I think that's a lawyer question you need to ask Harry Schwartz. Okay? I'm not a lawyer. What will it hurt to go talk to him?" he coaxed.

"What's to say he won't get us kicked out of the country?"

"I trust him," Mario said, and he did trust him. Still, he didn't know what Harry would do, if these people were illegals.

"My car was wrecked but my sister has a car. We'll meet you over there tomorrow at 4:30 when we get off work." She looked at the card. "At Brooklyn and Soto."

"I'll be there waiting for you, and I'll translate for you because he does-n't speak very good Spanish." As far as he knew Harry didn't speak any Spanish at all.

"Okay," Teresa said, "I'll see you tomorrow."

***

Mario ran all the way from school to be sure to be there in time, and had been early enough to churn through a couple of pages of Mrs. Maloney's extra credit packet. Harry had a couple of clients coming in, but promised that he'd left the afternoon open for Mario's prospects. In the meantime, Barbara had offered to proofread some of his homework. Mario liked that, because she marked wrong answers, and he was able to erase and put in correct ones. He didn't think anyone in his school had a secretary for homework. She even measured him for a sweater she said she was going to knit for him. She wasn't too bad, sometimes—not that he'd wear some sweater except to show her he was wearing it. He was too anxious to waste much time on schoolwork, or standing still for Barbara and her tape measure, and soon he was pacing the sidewalk in front of Harry's office. Finally, Teresa's sister drove up and let Teresa off while she went off to find a place to park.

Mario led Teresa inside to the waiting room. She sat stiffly on one of the many chairs and waited nervously for her sister to join her. The elderly clients who had been in consultation left. Barbara got up from her desk and took pictures of Teresa's bruised forehead—which looked much worse than it had the day before—and her sister's badly swollen arm.

Barbara told Mario, "You can go in now."

Mario interpreted for Teresa, and led them in to meet Harry.

"After this matter is finished, we'd like you to help us with green cards."

"Were all your kids born here? For a green card and eventual citizenship, that helps."

"Yes," Teresa said.

Harry asked for details about their husbands and children.

"I'm from Chihuahua, and so is my sister. We got over here. We each got hooked up with guys in the states. Their fathers are gone. The fathers were from Chihuahua too, so we're kind of stuck in the woods. Mario said you could help."

"I told 'em yesterday, these are lawyer questions. My promise was that we just wanted to do what was best for them," Mario translated.

Harry nodded. "Yes, we can handle it all. We will need their documentation. You can explain to them that everything they tell me is confidential. The law says that I have to keep the secrets of my clients. But first, let's talk about the accident."

He called Barbara in to request she bring forms for the car accident, and forms for the green card. She'd been listening, and came in with the paperwork. She looked at the piles on Harry's desk, and made two stacks in front of Mario, explaining which was which.

Then they plowed through the forms.

Mario went back and forth about the details of the accident, with Harry's questions and the sisters' answers: who was in the car, who was hurt, how they were hurt. Harry called Barbara in on the intercom again, and had her fast track immediate doctor appointments for everyone.

While Harry was talking to Barbara, Teresa looked uneasy.

"What are you going to get out of this?" Teresa asked.

"I'm just...I'm just the translator," Mario said, "Harry will take care of me. He doesn't pay me for the cases," he lied.

"I don't see what you get out of it."

"If any of your friends have an accident or need a lawyer, call me. If we get the case, you get twenty dollars. Tell your sister, tell everybody."

Barbara came in with more papers and more questions. Teresa and her sister filled out statements. Mario sat in on their session and translated between Barbara and the sisters.

Finally the newly signed clients were done.

"We have to pick up the kids," Teresa said.

"And go to your doctor appointments," Mario reminded them, handing over appointment cards that Barbara had handed him. He glanced at the date and time; they were scheduled that very evening. As they reached the door, Teresa grabbed Mario's sleeve.

"Thank you," she said.

She kissed Mario on the cheek.

Mario was humming with excitement, but maintained a calm, adult demeanor until she made it outside, and then he whooped and smacked his hand on the ceiling.

Adrenaline was pumping. He'd just nailed his first case with Harry. It occurred to Mario how much more interesting this line of business might be than working with Cosmo.

Chapter 4
1966
New Wheels and Deals

A month before his sixteenth birthday, Mario paid the new car dealer $4295 in cash. On his birthday, he got his driver's license, but had to wait several days for the insurance to be approved, since his birthday had the bad timing if falling in the no-mans-land week between Christmas and New Year's. On his birthday, instead of getting one of Barbara's badly knitted sweaters, Harry presented him with a business suit. A week later, he took delivery of a brand new, black with black interior, beautiful 1966 Chevrolet Corvette Coupe. When he paid what he and Harry Schwartz agreed was a highway robbery price for the insurance premium, he felt the insurance companies were getting back at him for the cost of so many cases he had already given Harry. He was sixteen with a sports car. The high premium was expected.

Frequently before they went to church, Mario and his aunt went window-shopping at Dearden's. When a new shipment of furniture came in, they "ooed and aahed" over it. Sometimes the favorites changed.

They walked through the store, pointing out this and that which they would buy if they had the room. Aunt Carmen picked out her favorite dining room set, a new bedroom set, and Mario picked out a new, extra big bed even he could stretch out in. He thought it best not to tell Aunt Carmen how he once had jimmied the emergency exit in Dearden's back, and snuck in with Pixie to try out the bed. It had been exciting but Pixie had made more noise than two cats in heat, and that was one experience he didn't care to repeat.

On just such a day, they were driving from Dearden's. They passed one of the taller corner girls who was walking into Hollenbeck Park. Mario couldn't help admiring her legs. At a glance, he recognized her. It was his special friend Pixie, who still had coltish legs, and skinny arms but was putting on a little weight in her middle. He wondered if he should mention karate classes to her as a means of keeping fit. That's what Cosmo would be sure to say. She kept a terrible diet, living mostly on fries and chips and candy. Aunt Carmen didn't notice her; she was checking her permed hair in the mirrored visor.

As he turned into the parking lot, Mario saw Carson walking with a couple of his sisters toward the church. Mario waved and pulled up in front of them. He got out to open the door for his Aunt Carmen. Mario could feel the eyes of Carson's sisters on him. He saw to his satisfaction that Aunt Carmen was wearing something new and store-bought. Now that he was the man of the house, gone were his aunt's days of patched faded dresses. Aunt Carmen pushed down the door lock. Mario unlocked it before he slammed the door shut. He started toward the entrance.

"You should lock it, Mario. Someone will steal your radio." His aunt stopped in the middle of the parking lot, clutching her new purse and refusing to move until he answered her. A dry wind blew and she reached up and clamped her hat on her head.

"No," Mario said, walking back to her, "I don't want to. I always leave it unlocked."

He waved at Carson who was across the lot in the herd of his sisters and their friends, but close enough to hear the exchange.

"He doesn't want anyone to break his window to get at the radio," Carson said, sounding a little envious. The girls twittered as if he'd said something clever.

It occurred to Mario that if you collected the brains of all of Carson's sisters, there might be enough there for a normal girl. They were nice enough, but no geniuses.

"That's right," Mario said, "I don't want any gangie to bust up my car just for a radio. So I leave it unlocked."

Carson had developed his body shop relative but hadn't stopped there; he'd also developed good contacts who sent him cases regularly. Carson would line it all up and then meet Mario at Harry's office with the people who had the accident. If the case was good, Carson immediately got his cut from Mario. Mario made sure he always had a lot of cash on him to grease all the hands necessary to keep his volume of cases up. He had everyone looking for cases, even the people who signed with him. Word of mouth from the accident victims was turning out to be the best referral source. They loved the cash kickbacks that he gave. Many times he paid for a case that he knew up front was no good, but he considered it to be an investment. Sooner or later that person he paid would call him again, probably with a good case. Already he was carrying wads of hundreds bigger than his mentor Cosmo.

Carson and Mario let the women walk on ahead into the church.

"You didn't drive from home, did you? Getting lazy in your old age."

It wasn't even a block away. Everyone walked to church. It was a social thing.

"No, I took Aunt Carmen to visit her dining room set."

"Let's go in."

Mario shrugged and went in, Carson following.

He always managed to find a parking spot where he could keep an eye on the car, except here at church there was no vantage point. He wasn't worried too about the local gangs breaking in. The church had an old guy who watched the parking lot, but gangs from outside would make short work of him. The car would be a target for other gangs and maybe just plain jealous people right from his own neighborhood. He had earned that car. It was his reward to himself, because he never stopped working with people that had accidents. Mario gave the old guy a couple of dollars to keep extra watch on his car, but didn't stay for the whole service.

***

Ever since Harry had hired two Spanish speaking girls, his small office space was filled like a ten pound bucket with a twenty pound load. Even if he had wanted to hire more lawyers, there would have been nowhere to put them. Harry didn't want to move, mostly because he owned this small building, including the two rentals on each side of the store front. He was so busy with personal injury cases that it was almost impossible to do the wills and other paperwork that had served him so well in all his years of practice. He had a part-time paralegal now, and delegated much of that old casework to her. Nothing he had done before could compare to handling personal injury like he did now.

Chapter 5
A New Leaf

Harry's office was a beehive of activity. There were several small desks for the Spanish speaking girls. The desks had come secondhand from an office. The chairs the girls sat in were new. The folding chairs the new clients sat in were far from new, but sported a shiny new paint job. Each girl had a phone, a desk set, pad, pencil, stacks of forms, in and out boxes which were made of wire mesh, and they shared a second-hand filing cabinet that took up one wall. It too had been freshly painted. Between the new paralegal and the translators, even though there was much more work than before, the piles of files and folders had vanished from Harry's desk.

Mario was waiting for a client. He didn't have a desk, but he did have wire mesh in and out boxes on the top of the file cabinet against the wall. As he was waiting, he went through his mail and messages.

"Mario," Harry said. "How much money do you have left after paying for the car?"

"You need a loan?" Mario joked.

"No, I don't need a loan. How much do you have?"

"About twenty thousand."

"You should buy a house. There's a new area, Monterey Park, off Atlantic Boulevard and Brooklyn. Some beautiful homes in a place called Monterey Hills. It's close enough for you to continue going to school over here. Ten minutes from my office. But it's a whole new world over there."

"Are you moving there?"

"No. I have a home, you know that. You've been there."

Mario pictured that beautiful home Harry had in San Marino, near Pasadena, less than a twenty minute drive from the office. Mario clocked it once at eighteen minutes by way of S. Atlantic.

"But we've always lived in the apartment—"

"I'm sure your aunt would be thrilled with the change. I'd like to see you and your aunt move there. Your beautiful car would blend right in with everyone else, and not stick out like a sore thumb. I want to see you out of this neighborhood. You're moving up, and frankly, it's moving down."

Mario felt suddenly defensive. The neighborhood was very much part of him. It wasn't exactly Beverly Hills but it had made him what he was. Did he still belong? He'd managed to stay out of the gangs. His aunt's house was an oasis compared to the rest of the neighborhood. She deserved better. Hadn't he always said so? He was confident he could afford it. He didn't know why he hadn't thought of it before.

"So how much money would I need? I know where Monterey Park is. I've been there to talk with clients."

***

The day started with a meeting with Carson, who paid back his last five hundred dollar loan with six hundred dollars, late as usual. Carson wanted to borrow again. They negotiated the amounts, with Carson never letting on what the money was going to.

From there, Mario went to Pixie's for a little fun during Pixie's off hours. It was no time for a movie, but he got to wake her up. He left her tousled and tangled in the bed sheets wearing nothing but with a smile on her face. He'd have stayed longer but he had a meeting at Harry's. With Harry leading the way and his aunt signing the papers, the house deal closed and he was still seventeen.

But soon with the new year, 1967, he was eighteen. Five months later, he was still eighteen, and it was May, and he was a high school graduate at last. The only reason graduating was important to Mario was that graduating was important to his aunt. Real life was much more interesting, not to mention distracting. Most of the people he started school with had never made it to high school, much less through it. At eighteen, Mario finally graduated from high school. He was glad to be free of the classroom; but he'd just enrolled in the school of hard knocks. His lessons were just beginning.

***

It was a day of bad news. Mario had just heard Pélon had been sentenced to prison for assaulting a police officer. For years, Pélon had escaped jail time, but his good luck had finally run out. Mario made plans to visit him in prison and see if there was anything he could do for him.

It was just the beginning of a dramatic day.

The door opened. Instead of the client Mario was expecting, Pixie walked in. She was dressed in a red linen suit that looked like something Lady Byrd Johnson might wear. She flashed a big smile at Harry, but when she came up close, Mario could see she'd been crying.

"How do you do Mr. Schwartz?" Pixie said.

"Excuse us, Harry," Mario said. "Barbara, can you give me a buzz on the pager if Mr. Juarez comes in while we're out?"

Barbara agreed.

"Let's grab a coffee," Mario said. "And maybe a Danish. You're looking a little peaked."

"We gotta talk," Pixie said.

"I'm all ears."

The traffic buzzed around them. There were people out on the sidewalk, but it wasn't especially crowded. Pixie's bright red suit was conservative for her, especially at this time of day. She had slightly slanted eyes, and a wealth of silky, straight brown hair that cascaded down her back. Mario had never seen her in the daylight without her signature red lips and heavy eye-liner, fake eyelashes and brightly colored cheeks, but he thought beneath all that, she was probably a very pretty girl. She was tawny with big brown eyes, and built slim like a greyhound, not at all buxom like most of the other corner girls. In the time he had known her, she'd gotten so much taller, that her name barely fit. She was nearly as tall as he was, and he towered over everyone. She had been putting on weight lately.

"I can't stay long," she said, as Mario opened the door to the 24 hour diner. "This is usually my busiest time of day, but I just got back from..." she choked up a little, and got quiet.

After a quick glance at the crowd perched on the stools, Pixie passed up the counter where they frequently sat, and instead chose a booth against the glass storefront. The waitress, who recognized them, brought coffee before they'd even sat down.

"Hey Tilly. A Danish for the lady," Mario said, and he ordered steak and eggs for himself. It was afternoon, but steak and eggs were the diner's specialty. He didn't have much of a sweet tooth, although they served really great pie.

"Some milk too," Pixie said. "My stomach's acting up."

Tilly bustled off.

"What?"

"Remember last week when Nana insisted I go to the doctor? Well I did. And I went back today and they told me, the rabbit died."

"You're pregnant?" Mario's voice might have raised a little bit, but no one seemed to notice.

"Shhh." She put her fingertips over his mouth, and met his eyes. Her lower lip was trembling. She nodded. Tears spilled over, spreading black streaks down her cheeks.

"Mario, I don't know what to do. I haven't even told Nana yet. A baby is the kiss of death for a working girl. I just..." she sobbed. "I guess I have to get rid of it, but I just don't know. I'm so scared."

Mario put his hand over hers. He grabbed his napkin, dipped it in his glass of water, and dabbed her eyes with the cloth napkin.

"Hey, it'll be okay," Mario said.

"That's easy for you to say. You're not the one in trouble."

"I'll take you to Aunt Carmen. She's the expert on babies. She'll be able to help. She won't help you get rid of it, I know that for a fact, but she knows all about babies, and girls in trouble."

"Do you think so? Ladies who aren't in the life don't usually tolerate us, but I have heard good things about your aunt. She delivered Hershey's baby, but you know, Honey's been pressuring Nana to kick Hershey out."

The waitress brought their food and a glass of milk.

Pixie drank half of it, and poured her coffee into the glass, and finished the rest.

"I know so," Mario said. "Now eat your Danish before you and your baby starve."

A few moments later, his pager went off. Mario's client had arrived.

"Listen, Pixie, I gotta talk to a guy about a case, but you wait here. I'll be back in fifteen minutes, and I'll take you by the house. Aunt Carmen will be home then, and she'll know what to do." Even though Mario and many of the old crowd had moved on, and most of the corner girls had different faces, Pixie was still living with Nana.

After May, he was no longer spending all day in a classroom. He was able to spend most of his waking hours networking and working. Even after Dearden's was paid off entirely, all his time and effort bore fruit. He built his savings account back up at an astonishing rate. He convinced his auntie to quit her job. He gave her $150 a week spending money, and took over the household expenses. Almost as proud as his Aunt Carmen, were Harry Schwartz and his first mentor, Cosmo. Cosmo would shake his head and proudly say, "That's my boy."

Mario had $13,000 in cash and $24,000 at the Bank of America on First and Chicago Street. He felt like a rich man. He was happy as could be. Except for Carson. Carson made him miserable sometimes.

Mario wanted to bring Pixie to Carmen, but Pixie kept putting it off. She wasn't going to a doctor, but she was getting big enough for everyone to notice. Mario noticed, somewhat grimly, that it didn't seem to slow down her business any. He didn't want to be petty, but sometimes Mario felt a twinge of something. He didn't know if it was jealousy or what. He was trying hard not to be a hypocrite. Pixie swore up and down it was just a job.

***

Carson would never talk about anything except that Mario was making all that money while Carson was always broke. Mario joked around with him, and told him to go out and hustle more business and he wouldn't be broke for long.

Maybe Carson did have shifty looking eyes that put some people off, but he was still doing okay. Mario was bringing in about ten cases a week. There was an average of two to three people in his cases. Each case settled on how much the doctor bills were for each person making a claim of injury, plus loss of earnings, plus property damage for the owner of the car. The cases settled fast. Volume is what mattered to Harry. He had never made so much money in his life, and he was raking it in. Harry paid Mario more than he'd agreed on, rained him with bonuses since Mario did more. He didn't just bring in clients; he also ran paperwork sometimes, or translated, or, thinking on his feet, did other things that needed doing. Harry had been feeling old and fatigued. Before Mario had stepped in, he had been just plain tired. He didn't smoke or drink alcohol. Now he was jazzed, and the only stimulant was the excitement that that Mario had brought to his life by bringing him countless Latin families that had been involved in accidents. He started doing some of their regular business too, like drawing up wills which was more work for Barbara than it was for him. By now, he had another paralegal hired Barbara a paralegal to boss around. Space was at a premium. They were getting ridiculously crowded. Harry loved the hustle and bustle.

His reception area was too small. Now there were lines of people waiting to see him, wanting to sign up as a new case or to check on an existing case, or coming in to get their settlement money. One of his long-term tenants, an ancient tailor who was old enough to have made the sails on Noah's ark, finally decided to retire, and Harry jumped on the opportunity to expand his office on that side.

That helped some, but not enough. Soon after, his other tenant moved out and Harry expanded the reception area. Barbara was thrilled at the space, but even more thrilled that the Spanish-speaking assistants could graduate from used student desks to full size furniture and get their overflow off of her desk.

"Harry," Mario told him one day, "you spend all this money moving walls to make a bigger office, why can't you spend some money on the front of the building?"

"What's wrong with the front of the building? It's been like that for two or more decades?"

"That's exactly what's wrong with it. Harry, it's time you give it a face lift."

Soon after that conversation, there had been one of those little shakers LA is so famous for, and a chunk of the facade landed on to the sidewalk narrowly missing a client. Harry stepped over the chunk of concrete, and, grateful to have been spared a personal injury lawsuit, decided to invest the money from his insurance on refurbishing the storefront. When he was done, he had refaced the entire building, including the two remaining rentals.

By comparison, everything else on Brooklyn Avenue looked more shabby then ever. Those weren't the only facades that were going downhill. Mario learned it wasn't just buildings that had false fronts.

Carson had been doing a good job bringing in cases and selling them to Mario. Mario in turn was selling them to Harry with no problem. They were good cases. Sometimes amazingly good. Mario wondered how many connections Carson had, since he was bringing in so many good cases. He didn't think Chi's body shop was that busy. Carson was no longer the silent kid, though now at times, Mario wished he still was, since all he ever did around Mario was complain and ask for more loans.

Carson was a couple of months younger than Mario, and in many ways, younger than his years. He'd been coddled by his sisters and mother his whole life. He had no empathy, or at least, none that Mario could detect; and he didn't have Pélon's loyalty or intensity, or Mario's easy winning ways with people. All Mario knew was that, as agreed, Carson was getting clients from body shops that didn't compete with Mario. He didn't know where Carson was spending the money he borrowed, but assumed, optimistically, it was to grease the palms of his sources. At least he always paid back the money quickly. Carson had his own contacts. It was almost troubling, though. Carson must have been keeping a really low profile to be able to spend so much time on Vago's turf without getting shot. Or was something else going on? Mario didn't know.

Though he'd moved out of the neighborhood, sometimes he went back. He visited neighbors like Pélon's mother, Iris, and Señor Chapo. He even stopped by the church once in a while. He visited Nana's frequently, usually bringing a bag of groceries with fresh produce, peppers, onions, tomatoes, garlic, and various cuts of meat so she could fix the dishes she and Pixie liked. He had a sack of those groceries in hand as he crossed the street on the way toward Nana's ice-cream colored house, when right behind him, tires squealed, metal shrieked, people screamed. A second car must have been going faster than the car behind it. The cars glanced into each other, and skidded all over the road, knocking into posts, and mowing down trash cans all along the street. As the dust settled, Mario set aside the groceries. He ran to the cars, and started helping the injured, and was handing out his card to everyone he saw.

Dibble was not the responding officer; it was someone Mario didn't know. He told the police what he'd witnessed, but it hadn't been much since he'd been facing the wrong way. He didn't really see much of the post-accident activity since he ended up spending most of the morning holding the hand of a confused middle aged Mexican man who spoke no English, and who had to be cut out of his car. Ambulances came and went; and Mario heard there was a fatality, but had no idea who it could be. So he was completely shocked, afterward, when he arrived at Nana's house. Pixie, oversized belly and all, came running at him, flung herself in his arms.

"Did you hear? It was Nana! Nana died in a car crash," she wailed.

The funeral was held at the church. Nana had not been wealthy, and had not been allowed to attend due to her profession; but she'd been generous with the church, and now, finally, the church returned the favor.

The viewing at a funeral home resulted in a packed parking lot. The mortician had been one of Nana's clients, and they'd managed to hide any damage the vehicles had left. In her coffin, she looked younger and fresher than she had in decades. Some of the girls had brought Nana's favorite cookies and pralines from the Mexican bakery.

The funeral home had several rooms open; and most of the people in the other rooms had come to pay brief respects to Nana, while slipping from one or the other so they could hide their connection to a woman of such notorious character. The guestbook filled with fictitious names. The funeral itself was small and sad, with only the girls in attendance. Dibble had said he would attend, but at the last minute, had called it off to do something with his wife. Of all of them, Pixie was the most inconsolable. She'd grown up in Nana's house since she'd been taken in as the orphaned daughter of a woman in the life, and she had no one else in the world.

Probate had taken two months. Because of Mario's connection there, Nana had had Harry handle her business. Harry who was actually a very good and ethical lawyer, had breathed not a word of it until the day all of the corner girls showed up in his office for the reading of the will.

Mario was surprised at their arrival. He shook the girls' hands as they came in, but was on the way out to a meeting with another client.

"I'm scared," Pixie said.

She was all baby, but thin arms and legs. Mario wondered if she'd been eating at all.

"I'll be back after this meeting. Wait for me."

She said she would.

His meeting had taken longer than expected. The November nights were getting shorter, and the sun set, and Mario had to drive across town to get back to the office. When he arrived, everything was shut down and dark. Everyone had left, except Pixie, who was sitting outside on a pretty wooden bench that had been placed in front of the new storefront.

It was completely dark as Mario walked up; or maybe his eyes had been shocked by passing headlights. He did not see her there, but he could hear her as he came up, quietly sobbing.

"Pixie, is that you?"

The sobs quieted except for some hiccups and sniffles.

She responded softly, "It's me."

There were still cars driving after dark, and the noises of traffic continued. Mario sat beside Pixie.

"I'm lost," Pixie said. "Nana left everything to Honey."

"I can't believe she didn't take care of you," Mario said.

"Your Harry Schwartz said Nana expected Honey to do the right thing. And Honey did the right thing, the thing she wanted to do all along. She kicked out Hershey because of the baby. And she kicked me out. Not that I would have stayed, anyway, she's going to charge all the girls half of what they make. She's horrible. She doesn't care if everyone leaves. It will just make room for new girls." Pixie broke down again and cried on Mario's shoulder. By the time the storm was exhausted, Mario's eyes were accustomed.

Tears caught the light on the tips of Pixie's lashes.

"Dinner is out," he said.

He could feel Pixie take it like another blow.

"Forget dinner," he repeated. "You're coming home with me."

He unlocked the office, and made a quick call home.

"I'm bringing a guest," he said. "Please make up the guest room, and put an extra setting at the table."

As expected, his aunt accepted Pixie with open arms, but without a trace of sentiment. She took one look at the corner girl's ruined makeup, streaks of mascara running into rivulets of powder, and lipstick and gloss, and foundation, and dragged her into the bathroom where she took a washcloth to her. The girl who came out was one Mario scarcely recognized. She really did look like one of the girls from his high school class.

"I thought you were older," he stammered. "I always thought…"

"I'm six months younger than you," Pixie said. "You never asked."

Aunt Carmen stared at them both, but mostly at Pixie's young face. "When I think of what you've had to do all this time, just to survive… For shame, Mario. You should have brought her here long ago."

Gift of gab or not, Mario couldn't make a response, he was so choked up.

And later, after she had fed Pixie, and tucked her into the nicest bed she'd ever slept in, Aunt Carmen scolded Mario within an inch of his life. She chided Mario for not bringing her sooner. He took it all, even with a smile. When she could say no more, all he could do was hug her.

"They're all frauds at the church. All those finger-pointers who spout good deeds, promise hellfire, and do nothing. But that's not you," Mario said. "There's not one of them good enough to touch the sole of your shoe. All I want to do is make you proud."

Pixie's baby girl was born not two weeks later. They named her Elena.

Life could not have gotten stranger. It was the end to Mario spooning with Pixie in the morning, though she was living in his house. It was the end to visits to Nana's house, that was now Honey's house. The ice cream colors were painted over by a dark brick red. Most of the corner girls found somewhere else to go. New girls moved in, none of whom had known Nana, and all of whom forked over half of their pay. No one called them corner girls any more. They were all prostitutes. Dibble still visited, though he was no longer a newlywed. He didn't call them newlywed lessons any more.

Life went on.

Pixie had nothing to do except take care of the baby, little Lainey.

Carmen found out Pixie could barely read, and tried to teach her. It was while watching these efforts that Mario realized that all along, Carmen must have wanted a girl to raise. She had all that midwife history on her back to unload to someone else. Pixie was grateful to Carmen, and did her best, but even Mario could see the girl's bewilderment as she tried, in futility, to live up to Carmen's expectations.

At least one thing in Mario's life was constant. Harry's office was consistent. Mario spent more time there than usual, and he was there when Carson had walked in at dusk with one of his spectacular cases. Barbara groaned when she saw him, and muttered something under her breath about how much work Carson's cases were—she was still just paid by the hour. He never brought in an accident that didn't involve a carload of whiplash cases, which, to Barbara, always mean working late to make lots of quick phone calls for emergency doctor visits before the bruises—if there were any—faded.

Barbara's mutters got Mario thinking. Mario only occasionally had a case that had more than two people, but Carson's cases were always cars or trucks packed with passengers. Always. He wondered if something was fishy. Identical cases all in a row just looked too perfect. All of Mario's cases were completely different. How did it happen that all of Carson's cases were identical? They were all rear-enders. They all had insurance. Cars full of people complaining of their necks. He knew he was being paranoid, but just to make himself feel better, Mario knew he'd have to bring it up. It came to a head when, just outside the office, Mario confronted him about three identical accidents that he had already sold to Harry.

Carson saw him as he walked up. Their eyes met. Mario didn't ask. He didn't have to. He'd known Carson long enough that he could recognize the wary expression, the defensive stance, the pout.

"You're setting up these accidents." Mario stated.

"No, I'm not."

Mario didn't say anything. He just stared. The longer he stared, the more Carson fidgeted. He loosened his tie, shuffled his feet, and his eyes slithered from Mario's to a crack in the sidewalk.

"Look, what the hell is the difference? You don't need to know about it. That's why I've never told you. You're not involved. So what if they fill up their cars, and agree to get rear-ended? That's what insurance is for. Everybody wins. I'm not doing anything wrong."

"Yeah, you are."

"What do you mean?"

"This has gotta be fraud. This has gotta be jail time stuff, man," Mario said. "You're using my reputation with Harry Schwartz. Harry could not only lose his license, maybe he could go to jail. I'm not a lawyer but this sounds like it's stealing, it's fraud or something a whole lot worse. There's got to be a world of difference between capping a case that really occurred and manufacturing one. You just can't do that."

Carson gave up the attempt at an argument and tried throwing a punch.

Mario dodged it, tucked his chin, twitched his left side forward, lifted the heel of his left foot, and launched a jab that knocked out Carson. One of his front teeth clattered on the concrete and lay still. His friend lay there half in the street, bleeding at the mouth. Mario, looking down on him, felt nothing but anger. Carson lay flat on his back with eyes closed, then looked up. He propped himself up on his elbows.

"You know what you can do? You can take your lily-white halo and screw yourself."

"Find another lawyer to buy your cases, Carson, because I'm never bringing another case of yours to Harry. And forget paying me back on that last loan. I don't know what shit you're pulling with that, and I don't want to know. Find another patsy."

Mario turned his back. He reached in his pocket, dug out his keys, and headed toward his car. Traffic buzzed along the street, same as usual, but everything had shifted, somehow.

"This isn't over," Carson yelled. "Not by a long shot."

Mario walked away without looking back. A whole chapter of his life was over.

Or so he thought.

A few days later, after Mario had already gone to bed, there was a knock on the front door. Half asleep, he listened as Aunt Carmen—in her bathrobe and curlers—had answered. Her voice was muffled. He sat up in bed. There was a commotion of voices, and his bedroom door flew open. Cops streamed in. For once in his life, he was speechless. They almost didn't let him pull on jeans and a t-shirt, but Aunt Carmen was there, and insisted. Lainey didn't wake up, but Pixie heard the commotion and came running down the hall in her pink slippers, nightie and bathrobe.

"What's going on?" she asked. When Pixie saw Mario wedged between two cops, Aunt Carmen had to grab her and hang on for dear life to keep her from jumping on the policemen escorting Mario out.

Hardly knowing what was going on, Mario did not resist as they cuffed him and dragged him into the squad car. He heard the clink of cuffs, smelled the sweaty taxi odor of the squad car. One of the cops told him that someone had called the LAPD with an anonymous tip that Mario was dealing dope. The last thing he saw as they pulled away was Aunt Carmen crying as if her heart were broken. It was an image that tore at his heart, one that he'd never forget. Nothing felt real except the sensation that his life had come to an end.

Chapter 6
Arrest
November, 1967

His life was not over, after all, but it was a whole other world. Mario had visited Pélon before but had never been on this side of the bars. He got a phone number for Tony Gallo from Dwarte, the bailiff who finger-printed him in the East Los Angeles Sheriff's Office. Dwarte told him his bond was ten thousand dollars, and that he could probably get Tony to put up his bail—which would cost him about a thousand—ten percent. He'd probably have to have some collateral for the ten thousand bond. The shock was wearing off. He didn't have to be a genius to understand that the bailiff getting him a bondsman was the same thing as him getting a case for Harry.

How was he going to convince anyone that he wasn't in the drug business? What would he do? Everyone claimed they were innocent, especially those who were guilty. What a fix he was in. His car, the money in the bank, the cash he had at home and he had no way to prove what he'd earned hadn't been by selling drugs. If he told the truth, Harry would be in trouble. But how could he snitch on Schwartz? He couldn't do it.

First, he needed to get out of jail. He finally got to the phone, and called Gallo. He got the exchange, the answering service. The answering service made him wait on the line, but that was okay. If he hung up, they'd never be able to call him back. There were some pretty unsavory characters waiting behind him, but luckily no one told him to get off the pay phone. Fortunately, he was taller than most of them, certainly healthier. Pretty soon, he heard this really rough voice on the other end.

"This is Tony. I understand you're in jail. What's the charge?"

"I don't even know. I think I'm in here for something about selling marijuana. They found it in my car. They even towed my car away."

"All right, well slow down kid. So how much is the bail?"

"Ten thousand dollars."

"And where are you?"

"In East LA Court. Not the court but the sheriff's office. Somebody here gave me the card, told me to tell you it was Dwarte."

"Oh yeah, Dwarte will look out for you kid. So ya got a thousand dollars?"

"Well, actually, I do, I had to turn it in when I checked in here, unless they take it from me."

And Tony said, "No, they're not going to take it from you. And what about, you been here? Are you legal here? I gotta guarantee ten thousand. You got anybody to sign for you? Got any property?"

"Yeah, I'm legal. I was born in New York, I saw the birth certificate once. And my aunt's got a house that we have. Why do we need all that?"

"Well, because I'm putting up a ten thousand dollar bond, it's the same as cash."

Mario wanted to tell Tony that he had more than that in the bank, but he didn't. Maybe he'd charge him more if he knew he had more. Besides, what if he started talking about all of his money and they asked where it came from? What could he say?

Instead, he said, "Look. I just need to get out of here. Whatever you need, I'm good for it."

About a half hour later, he met Tony Gallo. Dwarte brought him out to the little attorney-conference room next to booking where he had been fingerprinted and photographed. Shit he had seen in the movies had just taken place in his life. It wasn't exactly a palace drawing room, but any place would have been better than the holding cell where he'd been rubbing elbows with guys that would even have scared Pélon.

After one look at him, Gallo said, "What the hell is a clean-cut kid like you doing selling drugs?"

Not knowing at this point that he was going to say this probably another hundred times, Mario said, "I wasn't selling drugs. I only smoked marijuana maybe a dozen times in my life. I don't even know how it got there. It wasn't mine. Somebody just framed me. Somebody doesn't like me. Somebody that's jealous. I don't know. What's the difference? I'm stuck."

"All right kid, I'm going to put you up. You better not run on me. Cause if I send a dog after you for not showing up in court, I'm not going to be a happy camper. You understand me?"

Mario wondered if he meant a real dog or something else. It didn't matter, he wasn't going to do anything that made anyone—human or canine—come after him. "What do you mean, show up in court?"

"That's what I'm doing, kid. I'm putting up a bond that basically guarantees that you're going to show up in court with a lawyer to represent you on these charges. That's what this bond does."

Court sounded frightening to Mario.

"When am I going to court?"

Gallo just looked at him patiently.

"We'll know in a little while. But whenever it is, you gotta be there."

"I never break my word. If you want, I'll even give you the ten thousand. I've got that much. Not on me but I got it." Maybe he shouldn't have admitted he had the money, but he was only eighteen, he was in jail and he was scared. He'd never lost control of his life before, and he did not like the sensation. He was terrified of what this would do to Aunt Carmen. And now Mario had Pixie and the baby to support, too.

"No, that's okay, give me the thousand dollars later. Stop by my office across the street. You can't miss my sign," he said. "And do you have a lawyer?"

Mario thought about Harry Schwartz. That could get really complicated—especially since Harry knew where the money came from. Mario was afraid that if he told the truth, it would send Harry to jail.

"I know a lawyer, but I don't think he handles this kind of case," Mario said slowly.

"Who is it?"

"Harry Schwartz."

"Oh, you mean up on Brooklyn? He's doing a lot of personal injury work, P.I. I understand. He's a good lawyer, he's been around a long time, but Schwartz is no criminal lawyer, at least, not in my lifetime. No kid, you need a gun."

Mario thought he misheard. "A what?"

"You need a top gun. You need somebody to go in there and kick ass to get you out of this."

Mario knew a pitch when he heard one. "Why, you know somebody?"

"Yeah, I know somebody. He's expensive but he's the best. He's a friend of mine—the best in Los Angeles. Come on over and talk to me at the office. And we'll chit chat."

They shook hands.

"And bring me my thousand dollars."

"I'll be there as soon as they let me out of here."

"Now they might take a couple of hours to process you out, but I'll talk to Dwarte here," he yelled. "Dwarte!"

Dwarte who had been waiting just outside, came in.

"Get this kid out, I'm going to write you a bond right now."

"You got it."

***

He feared the confrontation with Aunt Carmen, but when he went home, it was worse than he imagined. She didn't say a harsh word. Her worry was hard to take. She fed him. He told her he was about to go see a lawyer, not to worry. While he was in the shower washing off the LA sheriff's office, she ironed his clothes for him. They tiptoed around the house, taking care not to wake Pixie or the baby, who had had a hard night.

***

At one time Bunker Hill had been a fashionable area of Los Angeles. Now it was just a place for tourists to take the short ride up to the top and back to Hill Street. Jake's office was on Hill Street, in walking distance to the Hall of Justice where the Criminal Courts were located, not far from the Federal Court House where the lifetime-appointed judges presided in their court rooms. Jake's office was right next door to the Grand Central Market, and practically across the street from Angels Flight, a 300 foot tram that had been taking passengers up to Bunker Hill since 1901.

He was surprised to see that Jake's office was a storefront much like Harry's; so immediately Mario wondered why Gallo had said Jake was a top gun and very expensive.

Mario was greeted by a very pretty receptionist who sat behind a wall and talked through a little window with a glass door. The reception room had more than a dozen cheap chairs waiting for clients. After waiting for less than five minutes, the waiting room door flung open, and a stocky, younger version of Harry Schwartz appeared sporting a huge toothy smile.

"Mario, come in. I've been expecting you."

He extended a big hairy hand with a manly grip. On the way down the inner hall, Mario observed two offices behind the small area where the pretty receptionist sat. Jake stood at his office door and followed Mario inside.

"Sit down, Mario. Place is a mess, I have so many cases, and every case has a mountain of paperwork." The towers of stacked files on Jake's desk reminded him of Harry's desk when he first met him.

Mario parked himself in one of two chairs for clients and watched as Jake sat on a huge, worn leather seat that looked very comfortable.

Jake had a legal pad out with a pen sitting on top of it as if he were ready to take notes, but his hands were nowhere near it.

He said, "I came out of law school and went right to work at the district attorney's office. I stuck around there for fifteen years. I've worked on every criminal type case you can think of. I've been in private practice for ten years, and I kick ass."

Mario adjusted his position in the chair. It wasn't as low as those in Harry's office, but then most chairs were too small for him.

Jake noticed the squirming, and possibly mistaking it for impatience, asked, "How old are you kid? You're a tall mother."

"Eighteen," Mario said. "I was born New Year's eve, 1948, but I usually count it as January 1 since I'm a day away from being the same age as the New Year."

"What's the arrest about? Tony says you're a good kid, but that's what he says about everybody he sends me. Probably just met you. Gallo can't file, can't keep records, and looks like he came out from under a rock, but he's got a good eye for people. Looks out for his own ass though. He wouldn't bail you out without a lot of security."

Mario interpreted that to mean that Gallo sent him lots of clients. He already had noticed the bad impression Gallo's office gave, but that gave him his half-life somewhere between gutter criminals who felt safe coming to see him, and a strictly legit hammer like Jake. He decided if he ever had an office, it would be nice. He didn't like the look of some of the gutter-crawlers who'd been in line, or the desperate look of the families who'd come to bail someone out. Mario gave his short explanation about the arrest. The voice on the phone told him to come to his office.

He recognized that Gallo regularly sent clients to Jake; and strongly suspected that Gallo and Jake must have some kind of retainer arrangement between them. He knew Gallo must have made some kind of assessment of the case, just as Mario assessed the cases he passed on to Harry. He told himself he was mentally up for meeting this new lawyer, but he wasn't.

Jake was fast, his voice thunderous. Sitting across from him it was like being the target on a firing range; his words were rapid bullets. He listened to what Jake was explaining about penalties for drug possession, for selling drugs, and fine points of the law and a light went off. Mario made the connection in his head. He realized he'd been so caught up in his own personal drama that he'd let all thought of Carson's doings slide. Mario had a vision of Carson the day before, lying there on his back, his mouth bleeding after he punched him for jeopardizing everything with his screwy cases. Everything became clear. It must have been Carson who planted the drugs in his car, then got the cops in on it with an anonymous phone call. This was Carson, getting even.

What would Pélon say if he knew Mario had been sent to jail on possession with intent to distribute a controlled substance? What would Pélon do to Carson if he found out Carson had done this to Mario? Mario's hands became moist thinking of what Pélon would do to Carson to make him confess. He felt sick to his stomach, and realized the lawyer had said something. He looked up.

"Where do you work, Mario?" Jake repeated.

"I manage advertising for a Karate studio in East LA and I translate for a lawyer who has Spanish speaking clients."

Mario didn't mention the cases he was responsible for bringing to Harry. He didn't mention the ongoing money deals with Carson. "The attorney I work with has a busy practice. He keeps me very busy."

"You need to be straight with me, I can't help you unless I have the entire picture, everything. If we don't make a deal and you walk out of here and find another lawyer, you don't have to worry that I will ever tell anyone what you told me here today. You must know that I would be breaking the law if I did that. After all, you are working in a law office, you realize this, correct?"

Mario nodded, but was very hesitant as he listened to Jake's questions. There was something almost familiar about Jake. He looked at him like Harry Schwartz did. Even though he had years to get to know Harry, he immediately trusted Jake. Even with that trust, it was not enough to tell him about the arrangement he had with Harry.

To tell Jake about that arrangement could hurt Harry either with the State Bar or the authorities. Plus, he had given Harry his word that no one would ever know about their arrangement.

Jake asked him about what assets he had if any, at this age. He didn't expect to learn that Mario owned a new car that had been impounded. A car that he had paid for. An account he had in the bank.

"Where did you get the money, Mario? You couldn't have made it working part time while you went to school. I know how much certified translators make. Not that much. And you're not certified. Translating for Schwartz cannot be that lucrative. I can't believe you made it running ads for the karate studio. Explain this to me. Were you selling marijuana? Is this how you made the money? You can tell me, I don't care. I just need to know the truth so I can defend you. Like I told you when you walked in here, I was a district attorney for a long time. As a former DA, I can do things sometimes that other criminal lawyers can't, but we need to start off on the right foot here. You gotta tell me everything that went on. I don't give a shit if you're guilty of selling weed. Or selling dope. Or doing anything else. I need to know. You are entitled to a defense, Mario, guilty or not. Even if you tell me you're guilty, I'm going to go in and kick ass for you. I need to know the story. I need to know the entire, unvarnished truth."

Mario nodded. This was going way too fast. He thought about prison. He thought about leaving his aunt alone, and now with Pixie and the baby on her hands. He thought of Carson, and his stomach burned with anger.

He could never tell the whole truth. Maybe he'd already said too much when he told Jake about the money. He regretted saying what he had in cash, at the bank, how he'd made the down payment on his aunt's house. How he paid cash for his car.

He'd given Harry his word, long ago. He could never double-cross Harry. What if this lawyer sitting across from him decided to go to the state bar and get Harry disbarred? He couldn't take that chance. He'd just have to do his time. But he hated the thought of it. It wasn't like he didn't know people in jail. But he was no longer a juvenile. He couldn't drink legally because you had to be twenty-one for that. He couldn't gamble because you had to be twenty-one for that. But for all other practical purposes, he was legal. He was eighteen and he was in trouble way over his head.

A picture of his auntie flashed through his mind. She was as he had left her at her standing at her door looking out, putting a brave face on over eyes full of tears, and looking every minute of her forty-three years. He felt sad; he was ashamed that he had brought this on her. He should have found some way to use the discipline he'd learned at Cosmo's knee to resist the temptation of using his years of martial arts training for anything other than self defense. Carson was no doubt blinded by hate when he hit the ground. But even blinded by hate, how could Carson do this to him?

The lawyer leaned forward, and looked at him with eyes that were too sharp.

"So. Tell me."

"Look, I can't tell you the whole story because I gave my word to somebody that I would never divulge the business association I have with him."

"Business association! You're just out of high school. What kind of business association? It has to be shady if you have to keep it secret."

"Mr. Morton—"

"What the hell do you need me for?" Jake interrupted, sitting back, in his great big chair. "What do you need me for if you're willing to go to jail? Why spend any money on me? Just go to court, get a public defender, which is what they're going to assign to you, and tell them that you just want to 'cop out.' You don't have a record. I seriously doubt you will do much time, but you will do some time. You're not going to walk away without society getting a real bite out of your ass. If you're lucky, maybe a year in the County Jail, and not prison."

"But I wasn't selling drugs. I don't know how drugs got in my car."

"A year in jail isn't all you'll have. You're going to have something on your record, kid, that you don't want to have. You're going to have possession with intent to sell a narcotic. It's possible that your money in the bank can be attached, taken away, even your aunt's house is vulnerable if it is discovered your money was used as the down payment. I will call a friend and get a copy of the report. I should have a copy by tomorrow at the latest. From what you tell me, they found a bag of marijuana in your very expensive Corvette. You can't explain away that much marijuana, and claim it's for personal use. They will no doubt charge you with possession for sale."

Mario said nothing.

Jake tried another approach. "Where did you get the forty some-odd hundred dollars to get the car?"

"The same place that I got the down payment to buy my aunt a home in Monterey Park."

"And how much was that?"

"I think we came up with almost twelve thousand dollars."

"Who gave you that money?" Jake sat up.

"Nobody gave it to me. I earned it."

"Selling dope? Selling weed?"

"Mr. Morton, you have my word of honor. I have never in my life ever, ever sold any drugs. Not weed, or anything else."

"Did you use it? Did you have it for personal consumption?"

"No. It makes people stupid. I don't need stupid. I don't know where that bag came from."

"Then how did it get into the car?"

"I don't know. Somebody's trying to frame me."

Carson's face flashed through Mario's mind. The fucking asshole.

"Why? Isn't that paranoid? Who's going to be advantaged by framing you? You're just a kid. An eighteen year old kid, for Christ sakes. Was it some territorial thing? You were dealing drugs in somebody else's territory and they're pissed off and they planted this stuff in your car?"

"Maybe another kid," Mario said thoughtfully. "But how can I say? I don't know for sure. Mr. Morton, let me repeat, I have never sold drugs. I have never been involved with drugs. Have I smoked marijuana? Yes.

Am I addicted to marijuana? No. Can I do without marijuana? Yes. Have I ever carried marijuana in a car for personal use? I've never bought so much as a teaspoonful. Not a leaf."

"Well, I'm at a loss. How can I help you if I don't know? Who are you covering up for?"

Mario sighed. He thought about the twenty thousand dollars he had left at the Bank of America. He thought about the cash he had at home. Then he thought about his promise. He just couldn't. He just couldn't. He just couldn't.

Jake said, "I don't even know what to quote you. I don't even know what to charge you for this case because I don't know what I'm fighting." He scribbled Mario's name on the top page of the legal pad.

"Let me ask you some questions, okay, and see if you can tell me this. Do you have a job after school? Have you been working? Are you employed now?"

He had already asked these questions, but had not taken note of them. He was taking notes now.

"The answer to all those questions, Mr. Morton, is yes. To all of them. The same as when you asked me the first time."

"Okay, good. Let's start there. Where are you employed?"

"Well, I'm not really employed."

"What do you mean you're not really employed?"

"I don't get a set paycheck. Actually I get paid in cash."

"And who do you work for?"

"At age ten, I started working with Cosmo, with Brooklyn Karate."

"At age ten?"

"That's right. At age ten. And I worked with him until I was fourteen and a half. Then I went to work with someone across the street translating when I was needed."

"You did translation work with Harry Schwartz. Is that correct?"

"That's correct."

Mario wondered if he'd fucked up by bringing it up. But he did do translation work. That shouldn't be a big deal. No one could ever prove that Harry paid him for cases. Even he could not prove he was paid for cases because he got paid in cash.

"Look kid, call me tomorrow. Here's my card. I'll make sure the call gets through to me or have them beep me. And I'll call you back where ever you happen to call me from. And then we'll talk more. I need to see this police report."

"So you want me to give you some money now? I brought a couple of thousand dollars, I just wasn't sure just what you—"

Mario was accustomed to reading people's reactions. Jake gawked when he heard the "couple thousand" but tried to cover it up.

"Save the money kid. I have no idea if I'm gonna charge you two thousand dollars or everything you have at the bank and at home. I don't know what kind of case this is because you refuse to give up a source. That's fine. I hope this person, whoever the hell you're covering up for is really, really grateful. I imagine it's some drug dealer."

Mario looked him straight in the eye, wondering if Jake would defend him sincerely, or if he was just in it for the money. Jake didn't look away, but now he had his poker face on, and that didn't tell Mario anything.

Mario took a deep breath, and admitted, "Mr. Morton, when I was a little kid, I might have hid dirty magazines where my aunt didn't find them. I might have had a beer or two before I was eighteen. I might have gone all the way with a pretty girl long before I was out of high school. But I don't lie. I have had nothing to do with narcotics sales, marijuana sales or anything else. I just told you that I was framed. While you were talking, it might have occurred to me who could have done it, but I don't know for sure. You need to believe me if you're going to be my lawyer."

When he went home, he was more unsettled than ever. He wasn't accustomed to people not believing him, and he found it disturbing.

Harry had told him to relax a few days, and stay home, but he was restless. Aunt Carmen had her hands full, keeping Pixie's hands off Mario, but she had no problem coming up with projects to keep Mario busy. She had a million things she wanted to do to the new house, and she used them to distract them both. She badgered him to join her at the hardware store, and they ended up bringing home a bunch of tools that he didn't know how to use.

Auntie solved that with a phone call. Señor Chapo came over, though how much help he was, was a matter of opinion. Still, there were walls painted, furniture relocated, stones laid, compost sorted, plants planted, grout bleached, toilets plunged, doors leveled. The list went on.

The next day, Mario called Jake's office. He couldn't resist.

"Kid, I haven't had a chance to check. I don't have the report. Give me another day, I'll talk to you. Call me tomorrow."

***

Before he left, Jake checked his notes from his meeting with Mario the day before. Jake was eventually heading to East Los Angeles Courthouse, but had purposely left early to give him time to make a stop. He hadn't been down these streets in a while. He drove down Brooklyn, saw the crumbling facades of the buildings. He had trouble even finding the street numbers. Parking was a nightmare. He was a little anxious about even driving his car through the neighborhood, much less leaving it in a lot or on the street. He'd be lucky to still have hub caps when he got back to it.

He found the karate studio. The front was as well-kept as a shabby building could be. He went inside, noticing the starkness of the place, but also that it was meticulously clean. It smelled of wood polish, pine cleaner, and sweat.

A dozen students were being led by an older man he imagined must be Cosmo, and a second class of nine younger students were working in a formation perpendicular to the other class, and being led by an intense young boy. Both leaders performed moves, calling them out, and the students echoed them individually, then put them together in a sequence. After everyone had seen the move, both leaders watched their respective classes performing the sequence, then walked among them, checking postures and changing their positions, the angle of a hand here, the width of a stance there.

He couldn't for the life of him figure out what it was that Mario had been doing here. The boy was fit. Maybe he was just taking lessons. Maybe he had been a trainer, like the boy leading the group of nine. What other job could this place offer?

The little Oriental man who must be Cosmo noticed him right away. Cosmo did a double-take at the Rolex, and the pricey gold and sapphire cufflinks. He turned back to his students, and set them to follow the other leader's exercise before he approached Jake. He was an elderly man, but one who moved easily with perfect posture. He bowed.

Jake bowed back. He creaked.

"Good afternoon, sir. My name is Cosmo. How can I help you?"

"So you're Cosmo." Jake cleared his throat, and identified himself. "I'm Jake Moreton."

"Yes, I'm Cosmo. What can I help you with? You want to take some training? You interested in self-defense?"

From the way Cosmo was assessing him, Jake suddenly felt middle aged, and unfit. He looked down at his paunch. Maybe he had put on some weight in the past couple of years. At least he was taller.

Jake cleared his throat, unsure of how to begin.

"Cosmo, I understand that Mario Luna works—or worked for you."

The mention of the boy's name drew a big smile to Cosmo's face.

"Yes, Mario Luna. A fine young man. Why do you ask?"

"Well, I'm his attorney."

"Attorney? Is he in trouble? Why would he need an attorney? I haven't seen him today, but—"

"Well, I could say that he's in a little bit of trouble."

"Trouble? Mario?" Cosmo drew himself up straighter, looking shocked. "That's not possible. What kind of trouble?"

"I can't get into that right now."

"What's he in trouble for?" Cosmo frowned. "There's no way he did anything wrong. I've never seen a more responsible boy. I know men who could take lessons on responsibility from this kid."

This whole-hearted defense raised Mario up significantly in Jake's estimation. The kid had earned at least one loyal friend.

"First, answer my questions, then I'll see how much I can tell you. The problem that I have, Cosmo, is that so far, I don't even have a police report. And I don't want to be spreading what may be a rumor."

"A police report!" Cosmo sounded truly shocked. "Mario? Are you sure we're talking about Mario Luna? Not that friend of his, that Pélon? Mario has no business in jail!" He got very agitated, then walked rapidly over to his chair and grabbed his coat as if he were going to run out the door that very minute. "I'll get him out."

"No, he got out of jail right away. He's already out on bail. He doesn't even know I'm here. I've already said more than I intended to. I'm on the way to the courthouse in East Los Angeles on another matter. I thought I'd stop by and meet the mysterious Cosmo that he talked about. He said he worked for you?"

"Yes," Cosmo agreed, suspiciously.

"Cosmo, let me tell ya, there are allegations against him—"

"That's crazy!"

"Well, then help me here, so I can help him. Tell me about him."

Cosmo did tell him. He didn't talk about catching Mario and Pélon spray painting his back wall, or seeing what he had thought at the time was a homeless boy sleeping in an alley, but he started with how he had hired Mario eight years before, when he had been going door to door looking for work to help out his aunt.

It wasn't a welcoming conversation accompanied by tea and cookies. It was a suspicious one, punctuated by pauses, and assessing glares.

Cosmo, who was the most courteous of men, did not go to his desk and offer Jake his single chair.

Jake stayed in place by the door, and threw in the occasional question.

"He would have been ten years old when you met him?"

"That's right. He was ten years old when he started working for me. I was about to go under. No students to speak of, after years here. Ten years old, and he walks in out of the clear blue sky and asks for a job. The next thing, he is out hustling business for this studio. It's been busy ever since. Word of mouth kept us going. Mario's mouth, even after he quit working here, and went across the street to work for Harry Schwartz. Not only did that boy send me ten years worth of customers, he made it possible that I could retire tomorrow if I want to."

"I know Harry. I don't know him all that well, but…you mean the lawyer that does—"

Cosmo pointed across the street.

"That Harry."

Jake looked over his shoulder, noticed how much nicer the building was than the rest of the street, then looked back at Cosmo.

"Yeah, he's been here many years. He's right there."

He pointed again across the street at the office building where all of the rentals had been combined into one law office, by far the finest building on the street, though that wasn't saying that much.

"You see that business over there, Mr. Jake Moreton? That was just a hole in the wall where Harry Schwartz practiced law. Until he met Mario."

"Mario works for Harry now?"

It's exactly what the boy had said. Jake looked across the street where lay the answer to the rest of his questions.

"Yes," Cosmo said.

Jake must have looked triumphant or something. However positively he reacted, Cosmo suddenly looked equally negative.

"Did I say something I shouldn't have?"

"No, Cosmo, you said something you should have said. But what exactly does Mario do for Harry?"

"Didn't Mario tell you?" Cosmo squinted up at him narrowly, more suspicious than ever. "Are you sure you're a lawyer? How do I know you're on Mario's side?"

"I am a lawyer," Jake reached in his pocket for his business card. He held it out. Cosmo made no move to take it.

"If I decide to take the case, I'm Mario's lawyer. So? What does Mario do for Harry?"

"Let Harry tell you."

"I don't understand why Mario's keeping this a secret. What's the big deal?"

"If it is such a big secret, I don't feel right telling you this. Besides, how would I know? I'm just an old karate teacher."

"Jeezus, the world is filled with secrets," Jake said. "Cosmo, thank you. You've been very helpful. At least I understand more than I did." He turned to go but paused standing half in, half out, as if the words had just sunk in.

"How old did you say he was when you met him?"

Cosmo said distinctly, "Ten."

"And he got you business at ten?"

"Sure did. And continued ever since. I used to want to pay him a percentage of what I made—two dollars a class. Now I charge ten dollars per student per class. But you know, he wouldn't take the percentage because he didn't understand percentages. For a while, I paid him a flat fee. Then I paid him a dollar every time one of his referrals took a class. Look at my calendar. They are all his referrals. The only reason these classes are so small today is there's a tournament going on, and I don't go to the tournaments any more. My students still do." He pointed at the back wall. A trophy wall. Shelves of them.

"Mario is a whiz at bringing in business."

"If Mario got you business at ten, at eighteen, he's probably doing the same thing for Harry."

Cosmo would not confirm it.

Jake looked at his watch.

"I'm running out of time. Let me run over to talk to Harry. Don't tell Mario right away that I've come. I haven't been retained by him yet."

Cosmo frowned. "You are on his side, aren't you?"

"If I take the case, I am," Jake said. "I'm not the prosecutor, if that's what you worried about."

"If he needs money, I'll help him." Cosmo reached for his wallet.

Jake waved it away, "Thanks, Cosmo, I'll let you know. You've been very helpful."

They shook hands. They bowed again. Jake's back creaked again.

"Some lessons would take care of that," Cosmo said.

Jake walked across the street, much the same as Mario always did, instead of going to the corner at the crosswalk and signal. He crossed right there on busy Brooklyn Avenue, dodging cars. Dibble wasn't around handing out jaywalking tickets.

It was brave. Brooklyn Avenue drivers had to be the worst drivers in the world.

Typical LA drivers.

Harry Schwartz's office had a low ceiling that spoke of the building's age, but it had clearly had a recent functional remodel, the kind done by an economical architect, not a decorator. Jake could still tell by the load bearing columns and beams where the walls of the original offices had been. The walls were freshly painted, and several shiny new office warehouse-style desks were manned by numerous shiny new secretaries of different ethnicities; Japanese; American; Latin. Each secretary was surrounded by chairs full of mostly like clients. The reception area was buzzing with activity. The one receptionist who was anything but new asked him who he was, who he wanted to see.

"I need to see Harry Schwartz. Here's my card."

The harried receptionist barely looked up.

"Oh, okay, but he's really busy. "

"Just tell him I'm here. He'll see me. I haven't seen him in a long time. You guys were just doing wills back then. You're doing something else now, I see."

While the secretary muttered into the intercom, he observed the motley collection of clients waiting in the reception area. There were a lot of secretaries working away, and none of them looked like they were dealing with probate. Most of them were speaking in low tones, in Spanish. Some were Oriental. This place had grown. It was clearly prospering. He wondered what had brought about the change.

Harry emerged from his office and caught sight of Jake. He crossed the distance with his hand out.

Jake looked past Harry where he could see a large Hispanic family being handled by a girl asking questions in rapid fire Spanish and jotting down the answers.

"Jake, Jake Morton," Jake accepted the handshake.

Harry greeted him as if he remembered him.

"Long time. Harry, I haven't seen you since…what conference was that, anyway?"

"I don't remember exactly."

"How's the wife? Jane, was it?"

"She died several years ago," Harry said.

"I'm sorry to hear that." Jake paused out of respect, then smoothly moved on. "Harry I'm not going to take much of your time. I gotta be in East LA. Court before Meyer. You know what that will entail if I'm late. Let me talk to you for five minutes."

"Sure. What's going on?" Harry glanced back at his office and shut the door.

He led Jake into a small but nicely furnished meeting room. "Have a seat."

The dark paneling was not to Jake's taste, but he was too tactful to say it.

"Not bad," he said.

"Just remodeled," Harry said. "But this wood was original so I kept it. So what is all of this about?"

"I'm here to see you about Mario. He was arrested for dealing—" Jake was on the verge of running through the high points of Mario's story, but Harry interrupted.

"What? No!" Harry was indignant. "Mario doesn't peddle dope. Mario doesn't peddle anything but Mario."

Jake felt a quick flush of something. Intuition, maybe. Between Cosmo and Harry, his gut was convinced the kid really was innocent of the charges. His brain wasn't that gullible though. He leaned across he smoothly polished surface of the conference table and speared Harry with his eyes.

"Ok, bottom line. I was across the street with Cosmo. He told me the story of how he met ten year old Mario. How he drummed up business. Like he's some kind of kid miracle. But Mario wouldn't tell me, and Cosmo wouldn't tell me what an eighteen year old kid has been doing for you. You know, I could care less what he was doing for you, but I need to know he wasn't peddling dope."

Jake stopped talking as the oldest of Harry's secretaries poked her head into the conference room.

"Mr. Elvia is on the phone," she said. "Do you want to take it in here?"

"Not now, Barbara. Take a message and shut the door behind you."

Jake almost laughed aloud as Barbara rolled her eyes at her boss. She clearly wanted to hear what was going on, but finally, reluctantly, shut the door.

"Of course he wasn't peddling dope. What do you mean he wouldn't tell you?"

"Mario says that he translates for you. But that boy must be doing a hell a lot of translating, considering how much cash he's spent, the car he drives, the house his aunt lives in, the money he's got in the bank. I could go on."

Harry sighed, and looked down at his crossed hands.

"Off the record, Jake, off the record."

Harry turned his chair and faced the window, where there was a clear view of a bustling crowd of kids walking into the karate studio. Through the glass, it could be seen that students were getting ready for their class and other students were leaving. Two little ones ran at Cosmo carrying trophies. Cosmo took the statues and put them on his trophy wall, handling them as if they were made of precious gold. Then he bowed low, to his students, and the little ones bowed even lower. He was standing like an oriental statue at the back of his building, the picture of patience and wisdom.

"Just look at that. More winners. Some years back, some eight years ago, I had a lot of time on my hands, and I watched Cosmo over there, sitting around his empty studio doing nothing except drinking a lot of tea. Then I sat here day in day out, doing probate work, watching Cosmo's business get better and better. First it was a class every few days, then a class every day. Pretty soon, it was classes back to back, adults in the mornings, then kids from three or four when the schools got out, sometimes to as late as ten. You've never seen such a turnaround. You should see the weekend classes in the alley. It's like the circus came to town. So I called Cosmo to find out about his magic bullet. I didn't believe it myself when Cosmo told me about this kid. According to him, the kid could do everything but walk on water. I was tired of handling all these damn wills and civil litigation that didn't pay me anything. I wanted to do what everybody else is doing. I wanted to do some serious P.I. What did I have to lose? I didn't have a clue how this kid could help me. But I went over there and I told him if he could help me, I could help him, and—you know, exactly what he did for Cosmo, he did for me."

He cleared his throat as if he were getting choked up.

"I wish you could have seen this office when he started. He wasn't even fifteen. It was just Barb, that nosy receptionist." Harry glanced at the door and raised his voice a bit. "Barbara, that nosy receptionist out there—"

Jake chuckled a little as under the door, he saw the shadow play of someone's footsteps quickly retreating. She had been listening.

"Barb, who is also a paralegal, and me. That's all there was. Now that Mario has been here a couple of years, I employ fourteen people, primarily because this kid went out and drummed up personal injury cases. The boy went out, made friends with people, met everyone at the body shops, ambulance drivers, priests, even cops. Because of that kid, I have translators on the payroll. I have secretaries. I have paralegals. Heck, my paralegal even has a paralegal. The cases started tumbling over, and snowballing, and I started getting referrals and…it's a long story. The kid never met a stranger, and never forgets a friend. So I pay him for bringing me these cases. As I say, this is off the record. A lot of us do it. No one wants to talk about it. Let's just call them referrals."

"Of course, of course," Jake said, "I don't give a shit if you're paying him. So, how much have you paid him?"

"Over the years, thousands. The kid bought a house in Monterey Park for his aunt. He's driving around in that new car. I know he's got money in the bank. He carries a big wad in his pocket to grease the people who are sending him cases. The kid was a grown-up at ten. Don't even look at his age. You should have seen what he was like when he was fourteen."

"What was he like?"

"The same as what you see now. I think he was born grown. The kind of young man if you threw him in the shark tank, he'd come out of it without a scratch, with a full wallet. No bloodshed anywhere. All the sharks would come out carrying Mario's business card. Kid can do no wrong."

"What are you talking about? So he's promoted business? How much business?"

"Officially, he's a consultant. Sometimes a translator. Spanish, like he said. And I can't tell you how much business, because I'm not sure. But I just told you I paid him thousands of dollars."

"So what you're saying is you made him promise he wouldn't tell. Because he didn't say anything. He was willing to go to jail rather than tell what he does for you."

"I didn't make him get up and take an oath, I just told him once, I guess it was back in 1963 or '64, that lawyers get into trouble with the state bar—they can get disbarred for people referring cases and in turn people getting money for them. That kid…" Harry suddenly got so choked up that Jake was a little embarrassed.

"That kid has more integrity in his pinky finger than anybody I know." He cleared his throat. "And he brought more than business into this old office. He brought life." Harry caught himself being sentimental, and snapped, "Do I need to write a book for you?"

Jake stood up. "No, not at all."

"Now look," Harry said, with a measure of self-preservation, "What are you going to do with this information?"

"I don't know."

"I'll be cooked if you use it."

"No, I'm not going to use it. I'll find a way to help this kid."

"This is the most honorable young man I've ever met in my life."

"Honorable, maybe, but, he was bending the law for you, so no saint. Where does he get his cases?"

"Oh, he's got a chain of people and professions where he gets his cases from. Like I said, the kid never met a stranger. Body shops. Emergency rooms, tow drivers. You know. But they're all good cases. The cases are—for the most part—Latin. Some Japanese. He gets 'em everywhere. He's got his card out everywhere. Beeper's going constantly. He finds these people. One minute strangers, then they're like his family, like they were long lost brothers and sisters and mothers and fathers. I've seen this kid cry when signing up a case, here in the office. Cry, identifying with a mother who lost a child."

"Con job?"

"He's just a kid who comes across as all heart because he is all heart. Have you met his aunt yet? The apple didn't fall far from that tree. Has he retained you?"

"No."

"Well, you just tell me how much, and I'll pay it."

"Yeah, I should make you pay it. But I have something else in mind. What if it cost you Mario?"

Harry didn't look too happy at that. "What is this? Blackmail?"

"Not at all. Look, if I get him off this thing without talking about where this money came from, don't you think they're gonna watch him? Don't you think they're gonna be around here and put two and two together?"

"Well, I don't know, I'm not sure about that."

"Harry, you paid him thousands of dollars in cash. If this case doesn't ring bells with the County District Attorney, I'll eat my hat. If, or I should be saying when, the Feds step in, both you and Mario will have IRS issues. If the cash you gave him is in your tax returns, then you are off the hook with IRS. Then all you'll have a problem with is the State Bar. But as for Mario, I bet my last dollar the kid has never filed a tax return ever. So he's cooked. We're talking about tax evasion, even if his lapse occurred when he was a minor. He's an adult now."

Harry looked troubled. "I should have had my accountant handle his taxes. I never thought about him getting in hot water."

"Too late." Jake said. "I'll be in touch Harry. It's not like you did anything strictly illegal. Unethical maybe, but not unorthodox. Most lawyers do something like this." Jake leaned forward and whispered conspiratorially, "If it makes you feel safer to hear it, you didn't do anything that I wouldn't do myself."

"Unless things have changed and the LA Times is wrong, you're the top criminal lawyers in Los Angeles."

"Maybe one of the top," Jake said modestly, but he was flattered by the assessment.

"The point is—you want to jump from criminal to personal injury? You're a criminal lawyer. You don't want anything to do with personal injury."

Jake chuckled. "I do my share of PI. Sometimes I take a case here and there outside of my usual thing."

Harry's voice rose slightly, as he saw his good thing with Mario slipping away. The writing was already on the wall, but he couldn't give it up. "You want to do rear-ender business? I know better. Give me a break."

"Harry, I'm never going to give up my day job, my criminal practice, but I've always wanted to do personal injury. We get dull with just one specialty. Upward and onward, right? Just look at yourself. Are you still doing probate or wills?"

"I do my share of wills," Harry admitted. "I just do a lot more other stuff too."

"Just like I keep my criminal cases, and still, I keep an office just for personal injury cases referred by criminal clients."

"Yeah, but you don't have a mill."

"No, of course I don't have a mill."

"Why would you want him? I read about you all the time. You represent all these hot shots making big money."

Jake chuckled. "There's not enough money there Harry. You know that. There are bigger fish in the sea."

Jake glanced at his watch and moved toward the door. His expression registered the changes in Harry's office—the background hum of a couple of low-voiced translators, a busy undergrad assistant, clients waiting, a secretary and a paralegal juggling a ringing phone, and stacks of paperwork. Even Harry's clothes were better. Not that Harry could ever be called a snappy dresser, but at least he'd retired those clumsy suits that looked like something Buster Keaton had worn on the silver screen.

"You're looking good, too Harry, I don't remember the last time I saw you in court. But you're looking good."

Harry said, "Yeah. I hit the big time." He sighed as he pulled down on his vest which might have come from last fall's sales rack at Sears, and said, "I feel pretty good too. I tell you, before the kid, things were just really going south, not financially, but just—I had no ambition after Jane died. You know, my kid are grown. Every day I came into the same drab type of practice. Now—since Mario—I have a whole new crew, not one of them over seventy. Never know what to expect. Still pumping away. But the boy has been better than a pension. If I retired now, I'd still be set for life. Hell, let's be fair. Even my kids would be set for life."

"So you'd say that knowing Mario has done something for you."

Harry reminisced, thinking back. "He's done a lot for me in the past four years. What you told me today will do something for me for the rest of my life. There's a young kid over there facing jail who still won't give me up. A kid who would rather go to jail than to give me up, or go back on his word."

Jake shook his hand. "Ya got that right, kiddo. That's exactly what he's willing to do."

On his way out, that nosy secretary of Harry's was standing by the door with her back to him, blocking his way.

"Excuse me," he said. She didn't budge.

"Miss!" he repeated himself. "I have a court date to get to if you would please excuse—"

She turned to face him, pulling his card out of her pocket and tearing it into tiny little pieces. She took those pieces and ostentatiously dropped them into his shirt pocket, and patted that shirt pocket. Then she snarled.

"Mario is a good boy," she hissed, poking him in the pocket with her sharp little finger, "He did not sell any dope." She poked him an extra time for good measure and stomped back to her desk.

Jake's expression never changed. He turned coolly and left; he even waited until he was inside his car halfway to his office to dig the shredded card out of his pocket. Whatever Mario had or hadn't done, Jake realized, the boy had no shortage of friends.

Epilogue
Endings and Beginnings

Mario didn't know what Jake had done to get him off with a slap on the wrist, but he was grateful. Now, two years later Mario spent half his working hours for Harry, and half for Jake. Harry was threatening to retire. Mario had been trying to talk him out of it. He didn't want Harry to cool his jets, but Mario's candle was being burnt at both ends. He was as tired as a man his age could be. It seemed crazy to him that the only time he felt any energy was after taking a daily hour-long class with Cosmo. He was glad to come home and rest, and as he approached his door, hoped he wasn't walking in on another fight between his aunt and his former girl. It's not like he and Pixie could carry on under his aunt's roof. He opened the door cautiously in time to see the end of an argument.

"I can't do it!" Pixie threw the book down.

Carmen picked it up, and put it back on the table.

"Let's try again."

"I'm done trying!" She grabbed her coat, and ran out of the door.

"I'll go after her," Mario said.

"No, let her cool off," Carmen said. "Unless you really want to straighten her out. She's a piece of work."

"Speaking of work, you'll never guess who I saw at work?"

"Let me guess—Santa wrecked his sleigh, and showed up at Harry's."

"Santa's more of a Jake type," Mario said. "No, I saw Eleanor Candles. You know, the one with the hats. And the other famous one, Gladys, somebody. They both came in to talk to Jake."

"Maybe they were giving him fashion advice," Carmen said. "Did one of them pick out that yellow suit of yours?"

"Maybe," Mario said mysteriously.

"That girl just gets my goat, every time," Carmen said. "I know she can do it, but she just doesn't try."

"I'm tired," Mario said. He had already shucked out of his coat. Still, he stuck his head out the door and yelled for Pixie.

Pixie didn't reply.

Carmen sighed and rested her head on her arms. Lainey was asleep. She was two years old now, and a holy terror. She'd gotten into crayons and had scribbled them all over the white brick of the house. At least she'd kept the artwork to the back yard. Mario had already spent a weekend trying to scrub off the crayon, before he realized he'd have to paint over it. Maybe next weekend. And Pixie would come back when she cooled off.

"She found work at a food joint," Carmen said. "But I could show her so much more."

"If she can't do it, she can't do it," Mario said. "Give her a break. I remember how you nagged me about math. I still hate math." He put his coat back on. "You can be relentless, Auntie. I better go after her."

"Try The Venice Room," Carmen said.

"The place with the red leather booths on Garfield Avenue? They fix a mean steak, and they're not too far from here."

Carmen shrugged. She had never been much for eating out.

Mario didn't need to go far. He caught up with Pixie at the end of the driveway.

"Took you long enough," she said. "Aunt Carmen would try the patience of a saint."

"But you love her," Mario said. "You just can't help it."

"Yeah, I do. I just hate to let her down."

"Give her time," Mario said. "She'll let you be yourself. You can take the time to find out now who you really are. You got family now. Whether you want to read books, deliver babies, or flip steaks at The Venice Room."

"Do I?" Pixie asked, almost grabbing him the way she used to BC. Before Carmen. Mario hadn't decided yet if he missed that side of her or not. Pixie was a work in progress, but so was he.

"I could go for a steak," Mario said. "Treat you to a couple of rib eyes at The Venice Room? Play your cards right young lady, and I might even spring for dessert."

About the Author

George Hatcher is an entrepreneur with a gift for business and storytelling. Whether he's traveling the globe as a consultant for lawyers in high profile aviation crash cases, advising boxers, or at home with Molly amid the birds and cats in California, he's always got his eye on the next project. A longer bio is on his website at:

www.georgehatcher.com/bio/bio.html